Just a Few of the Exciting Revelations About the Royals Foretold by the Stars!

- The dangerous "themes" in Diana's chart that warned of her bulimia . . . and her suicide attempts
- The astrological aspects indicating that the sexual arena would make or break Diana's marriage . . . and why Di and Charles ended up in separate beds
- What signs showed that Charles would be powerfully attracted to both Diana *and* Camilla Parker Bowles . . . and why his desire for Camilla was stronger
- Why Prince Andrew was astrologically primed to fall in love, and how his choice of Fergie was more perfect timing than a perfect match
- What in Fergie's chart indicated she would keep her finger on the self-destruct button
- At what point Diana really called it quits, and how her chart predicted disappointment, suffering, and betrayal
- How the planet Pluto set the stage for marital disaster between Di and Charles in 1988 and again in 1992
- How Charles's brush with death while skiing in Switzerland was predicted in his chart . . . and how it put the final nail in the coffin of their marriage
- Why Diana may never find genuine sexual fulfillment . . . and what man could release her real passions
- *And many more inside secrets told at last in*

WITH LOVE FROM DIANA

WITH LOVE FROM Diana

PENNY THORNTON

POCKET BOOKS

New York   London   Toronto   Sydney   Tokyo   Singapore

An *Original* Publication of POCKET BOOKS

POCKET BOOKS, a division of Simon & Schuster Inc.
1230 Avenue of the Americas, New York, NY 10020

ISBN: 0-671-89186-3

First Pocket Books printing January 1995

10   9   8   7   6   5   4

POCKET and colophon are registered trademarks of
Simon & Schuster Inc.

Cover photo courtesy of Globe Photos

Printed in the U.S.A.

Acknowledgments

Hardly anyone receiving an Oscar leaves the podium without thanking all those along the way who have helped towards that moment. Likewise, an author always has a team of helpers to whom he or she is indebted. On this occasion I have to thank the following—and in alphabetical order, not in order of importance. Richard Blanks, Nicholas Campion, my literary agent, Anita Diamant, Christopher Hutchins, Cordelia Mansall, my editor, Linda Marrow, Liz Nocon, Melanie Odell, "Paul," Christopher Robinson, Gregory Watson, and, of course, my sons, James, Alexander, and Dominic, who yet again put up with a diet of fast food and short temper while their mother slaved over a steaming word processor.

Diana will be seen through the eyes of history as one of the great tragedies of our time. Like all prophets damned by their own country, her value as a change bringer, a transformer, cannot be appreciated now. Her mantle is to drag the monarchy, kicking and screaming if necessary, at last into the twentieth century.

CONTENTS

Curtain Up

This book came to be written almost by default. I had mused that I would one day write about the events of 1986–1993—perhaps another ten years from now—but, as I explain in Chapter VII, situations conspired to bring about that moment somewhat sooner. First and foremost this book is about setting the record straight. When, in 1992, the world discovered Diana's "true story," it also discovered Diana had found—or tried to find—solutions to her unhappiness through alternative therapies, and astrology. And along the way, the simple story that Diana had consulted me became embellished to the point that, according to author Nicholas Davies in his book *Diana: A Princess and Her Troubled Marriage,* she had arrived on my doorstep in a pair of jeans and floods of tears one afternoon in 1986 and had been consulting me daily ever since. Therefore, I felt the facts rather than the fiction of my association with Diana needed to be placed on record. And that ought to come straight from the horse's mouth.

Right up until the end of the seventeenth century, with the exception of Edward III and Charles I, there had been a tradition of astrologers at the court of British monarchs. Indeed, William the Conquerer chose December 25, 1066, to be crowned, not, as many historians have opined, because the date was expedient but because astrologically it was extremely auspicious. As Christmas Day is close to the winter solstice, the sun is at its lowest point on the horizon, and by choosing midday as the time of the coronation, the sun was directly overhead, reinforcing the already powerful Christian theme that "here was a King of Kings."

Charles II, who clearly had no intention of following in his father's footsteps to the scaffold, was advised by astrologer Elias Ashmole. Ashmole carefully selected the ideal moment for all Charles's speeches to Parliament, thereby eliminating the possibility of another Cromwellesque *coup d'état*. John Dee, advisor to Elizabeth I, was perhaps the most famous and respected of royal astrologers, and although his reputation as an alchemist led to a popular belief he was a sorcerer, at court he was highly regarded as an intellectual. Dee lived at the time of yet another great and influential astrologer, Michel de Nostredame (Nostradamus), whose prophecies may have as much to tell us about the twentieth-century British monarchy as they did of sixteenth-century France—as I shall disclose in Chapter VIII.

More recently, Edward VII, Queen Victoria's successor, consulted the famous Cheiro, and although Elizabeth Windsor may have little time for astrology and mysticism, the Queen Mother and Princess Michael of Kent have both had their astrological charts cast.

Like the Queen, the Prince of Wales may not be a devotee of astrology, but as a follower of the eminent psychologist and mystic Carl Gustav Jung, he is clearly aware of Jung's deep interest in astrology. And Charles certainly knew of my consultations with Diana, and according to sources close to the palace, he approved of and appreciated my help.

An astrologer, like any lawyer, therapist, or doctor, has an ethical duty to guard his client's privacy. What happens in the consulting room should never be disclosed—at least not without the client's tacit permission. My astrological peers have been outraged that my professional relationship with Diana has become a matter of public knowledge. And even more outraged that I have, from time to time, written articles and books about the royal family. However, until 1992, Diana's permission was sought and granted for every article or written comment about herself and the royal family. And this book has also been written with her full awareness.

What many people probably do not appreciate is the delicate balance I have had to sustain in regard to my loyalty, on the one hand, to News International, who employs me and has given me a wonderful platform for my work, and, on the other, to Diana as a client. A tabloid newspaper whose business it is to sell papers and increase circulation does not have much time for an employee who considers her more pressing allegiance to be one client—admittedly one rather important client. And when, in the summer of 1993, every tabloid newspaper was able to serialize a royal book, it would have taken a saint of an editor not to be ever so slightly miffed that, despite having the equivalent of the goose who laid the golden egg on his staff, his was the only tabloid without a royal scoop.

During the first two years of my employment with *Today* newspaper, my devotion to Diana was paramount, and it was only when she gave me clear signals that the bond of loyalty had been severed did I begin this book. Clearly I shall still be opening myself to intense criticism, but at the end of the day the desire to set the record straight overrode my reservations. And I hope that the frank way the material has been treated neither diminishes Diana nor paints her in obsequious shades of pastel. Likewise, I hope I have succeeded in showing the value of astrology in both a therapeutic setting and as a commentary on the times and a barometer of the future.

In spite of, or because of, the times we live in, when the computer has become god and we can walk on the moon instead of wondering what kind of cheese it's made from, most people still nurture a yearning for the transcendental. And astrology is a marvelous and unique blend of the mystical and the scientific. The positions of the planets at birth are astronomical fact, but astrology and astronomy part company when astrologers declare the planets have a relevance to human character and the unfolding of earthly events. As yet, we do not have a categorical explanation of how the planets affect human behavior, but we can trace the progress of history against the background of the planetary cycles and perceive there is a clear correlation—a grand design at work.

Certainly in the mid 1980s it was very clear to me that the transits of Saturn and the outer planets, Pluto, Uranus, and Neptune, were going to have an immensely destabilizing effect on the royal family in the early 1990s. And my gut feeling—that it would be the demise of the Waleses' marriage that would precipitate a chain of events irrevocably damaging to the House of Windsor—has been borne out in reality. What we have yet to discover is whether my belief that England is heading inexorably towards becoming a republic will also come to pass.

History will view this last decade of the twentieth century as a time when many old institutions collapsed—some because their foundations were rotten and others because they were inappropriate to the New Times. Somewhat ironically, it may be that the royal firm, having come to much the same conclusion, accelerated its own demise by actually trying to move with the times. When Charles was invested as the Prince of Wales in the summer of 1969, it was done with great pomp and ceremony. There was something both touching yet profound about the Queen placing a crown on her son's head, thereby initiating him into the mystery of sovereignty and at the same time releasing him from her "apron strings"—and granting him rather a lot of wealth and territory in the process.

But this event was something of a watershed, because by the time of the Queen's Jubilee in 1977, the royal family was no longer perceived as a family set apart from lesser mortals. The television cameras had invaded that sacrosanct space. The public had seen what went on behind palace walls and discovered the royals weren't that different after all. In retrospect, the decision—largely encouraged by Prince Philip, the Queen's husband—to create a more approachable image of the royal family has not served the Windsors well. The demystification of the monarchy has, in effect, made it redundant. The gods on Olympus may have had human characteristics projected onto them, but they were immortal, powerful, untouchable—not like other men. And it must always be thus. Were the gods to walk freely on the earth, wander into Harrods for a new outfit, or have half a pint with the locals in the Dog and Duck, they could no longer hold the projection of the people. And we only have to refer to ancient myth to remind ourselves that when the gods fell in love with the mortals, all sorts of mayhem ensued . . .

The image of the monarchy should be extraordinary, beyond the reach of ordinary people—something to look up to, even to fear. And there is no doubt that the scandals of the early 1990s have not only demystified the monarchy, but made it unworthy. And Diana has played a large part in the rise and fall of the Windsors. She may even be its Nemesis. After her arrival on the royal scene in 1980, she quickly became the priceless jewel in the Windsors' crown. But by the time of her withdrawal from public duties in December of 1993, the family could be forgiven for musing that it might be better were she to be locked in the Tower of London with the rest of the crown jewels.

To have met Diana, to have been there at a time in her life when she was floundering under the weight of her obligations and her unhappiness, has carved its signature on my life. And, as I pointed out earlier, eventually there became a need to write about that experience. When I had completed the last chapter of this book, I was already three months over the deadline set by my publishers and I found myself writing "Curtain Up," which I had hoped to take my time over, in a state of near frenzy. At the time, I was heavily into Mozart's *Don Giovanni*, which played on the stereo in my study almost unceasingly, competing against the sound of keys tapping on my word processor. And, in keeping with the laws of serendipity, upon reading the program notes, I discovered Mozart was so late with the delivery of this opera that the musicians in the orchestra pit were only handed the score of the overture moments before the curtain went up on the first performance. *Giovanni* is considered Mozart's greatest opera, and although I can hardly lay claim to this being a great book, it could be said to be a book about a great soap opera!

Some of the stories recounted here may have been told before—but they have not been firsthand accounts, merely reports from "sources close to . . ." Nor have other authors had quite the same set of extraordinary subplots to deal with. In many ways I have likened this book to Tom Stoppard's play *Rosencrantz & Guildenstern Are Dead.* In Stoppard's play, these two minor characters from Shakespeare's *Hamlet* have their own story to tell. We are led into their lives and view the ghastly and ghostly events of the Court of Denmark from their point of view— effectively, Hamlet becomes an accidental backdrop to the real drama of Rosencrantz and Guildenstern. In much the same way, I am viewing the events of the late 1980s and early 1990s from my unique vantage point. And I hope this not only sets an intriguing period of history in a different light but gives truth to the old adage that fact truly is stranger than fiction.

P.T.
May 1994

I

Setting
the Scene

"Hello."

"Oh, hello. Can I speak to Penny Thornton?"

"Speaking."

"Ah. This is the Princess of Wales."

It was a Thursday morning and I was taking the call on the phone by my front door. I remember leaning heavily on the wall to support myself since my knees no longer appeared to be made out of cartilage and bone but something resembling blancmange instead.

"Oh, how nice to hear from you," I chirped, as if I were accustomed to taking calls from royalty every day of the week.

Not that it was a complete surprise. I had already been asked on two separate occasions by the then

Sarah Ferguson and Prince Andrew if I would "do" Diana's chart. Nevertheless the call, when it came, caused a sharp intake of breath.

Her voice, of course, was distinctive. And it seemed that I had known her for years. The rapport was immediate.

It marked the beginning of a six-year relationship.

In a way, I *had* known Diana for years. Like most astrologers, I had charted her natal horoscope as soon as her date and time of birth had become public knowledge. But, unlike most astrologers, I elected to use her chart and that of Prince Charles for a book I was writing on the astrology of relationships. In fact, I had begun this book almost to the day of the wedding. Even then I was aware that this marriage could go terribly wrong. And much as I wanted to believe the fairy tale, I felt I could not compromise my astrological judgment. In my book, therefore, I reluctantly voiced my misgivings about the relationship—and the flaws as well as the strengths of Diana's personality. At the time the entire country, if not the world, was already head over heels in love with Diana and saw only a glittering future for the royal couple. Not for the first time, so to speak, had I put my money where my mouth was.

There is no great mystique or privilege attached to acquiring a member of the royal family's chart. As with any public figure, the date, time, and place of birth is a matter of common knowledge. I had always been a keen royal "watcher" and had often used the charts of Prince Charles and the Queen to illustrate points when I was lecturing or teaching. I had noted with some amusement that my chart made major links with the royal family's charts and assumed that this was the reason for my interest. But at a deeper level I wondered if I would, indeed, have a more powerful connection. When I first saw Diana's chart, with all its contacts to my own, that strange sense of "I wonder . . ." became a more marked sense of something beyond coincidence.

To begin with, the Palace Press Office gave Diana's time of birth as 2:00 P.M. on July 1, 1961, at Sandringham. But within a week or so, a new time of 7:45 in the evening was being given out by the same office. Now, instead of Libra rising, this same sign was directly overhead on the Midheaven of Diana's chart. And in place of airy and graceful Libra on the Ascendant was hearty, outgoing, and globe-trotting Sagittarius. Astrologers had some difficulty in realigning Shy Di with this no-holds-barred astrological persona described by the "new" Ascendant. But we managed. And soon, of course, she began to show the world what a trendsetter she was.

But before I launch into my first impressions about Diana, a word or two about astrology—real astrology. First and foremost an astrological chart provides a means of exploring the personality. And if we take the idea that who we are dictates what our life will be, destiny no longer becomes something that happens to us, but a creative and interactive process. Of course, I do have some other notions about the nature of fate, but these are better left until a little later.

From the outset I believed Diana to be a far different kettle of fish from the gentle and compliant image she radiated. Her July birthday made her a Sun Cancerian, which certainly fitted in with her role as a nursery teacher and her fondness for domesticity. But this was by no means the whole picture.

For a start, Cancer is no pushover by any stretch of the imagination. It may be an emotional and highly sensitive water sign, but as a member of the Cardinal astrological family, there is real grit to the personality and an ability to get what is most desired—usually by the most circuitous route. We could say that Cancer at its worst is manipulative, treacherous, and deceptive, even if these traits are only manifested in order to protect and survive.

But whatever the sun sign revealed—and, if we are being honest, sharing the same sign with a twelfth of the world's population is hardly the most important marker for character or destiny—the nuts and bolts of Diana were to be found elsewhere. Two key structures suggested that, far from being submissive and selfless, this was a young woman who was volatile, unruly, and capable of pulling the most amazing stunts were she to feel threatened or denied. This might be easy to say with hindsight, but a bit more of a challenge back in 1981 when Diana was merely an untouchable image that gazed out of a television screen or from the pages of magazines and newspapers.

At that time I wrote,

Perhaps the most dynamic feature of her chart, however, is a configuration involving the moon, Venus, Mars, and Uranus. Many astrologers have spoken in glowing terms about the independent, adventurous, and exciting flavor indicative of this alignment (which is not disputed), but perhaps a more realistic view should also be applied. This configuration is not likely to permit her to slip easily into a conventional royal role: It implies that she requires great freedom of self-expression and, despite her desire for security, she needs plenty of stimulation in the way of exciting and novel experiences . . . A moon-Venus-Uranus arrangement in a woman's chart usually produces several romantic encounters in a lifetime and an underlying pattern of emotional truculence . . . On the one hand she may bring a breath of fresh air into her relationships through the sheer force of her personality, thus never letting them stagnate or fall into dull routine. On the other hand, if her marriage becomes too restrictive, she will break out and seek new and more exciting horizons. As a future Queen of England, the latter possibility is unthinkable yet alone practicable —but then, twenty years ago, divorce for any member of the royal family was undreamed-of!*

I also noted that there was a dangerous theme in Diana's chart. This emerged from the placing of Mars—a planet of action—close to explosive Pluto and Uranus.

This combination presents a violent theme and suggests the likelihood of exposure to dangerous situations. It is highly unlikely that Diana would generate any violence herself, so this may be a reflection of Prince Charles's chart—certain features of his horoscope point to a love of adventure and danger.

At the time, my feeling was that Diana herself would not "own" her Mars energy and it would be projected onto the man in her life, Charles. (Mars is the male principle in astrology just as Venus stands for all things female.) And, if I am honest, I did consider that either or both of them would be the focus of a violent attack, whether this manifested as intense criticism or a physical assault, even some kind of assassination attempt. Certainly Charles's brush with death on the ski slopes of Klosters was an expression of this astrological theme. And in 1993 it was revealed that the IRA had planned to assassinate Charles in 1985. What I failed to touch on all those years ago was the self-destructive tendencies redolent in this Mars-Pluto connection. In retrospect it was a major oversight. Diana's bulimia is an expression of the rage and self-abuse that lurks within this intensely Scorpionic aspect. Having this connection in a horoscope does not mean that the individual will develop anorexia or bulimia or attempt suicide. But given the right set of circumstances (and a chart like Diana's—already chock-full of emotional disease), pitchforking into self-destruct mode is an almost automatic response to emotional pain. With the benefit of hindsight, it is possible to lay the blame of much of Diana's inner turbulence and her behavioral extremes at the feet of this Mars-Pluto contact, and its containment in a sea of astrological conflict. But more of this later.

Back in 1981, I also considered that the prospects for a happy marriage between the Waleses looked rather bleak. Nevertheless, I have to say that however dismal the connections between a couple's charts, whoever they are, love is the overriding principle. In other words, love transcends difficulties. So it was always an option that these two would find the magic formula to transmute the base metal of their relationship into a golden marriage. By sun signs alone, the couple promised to be a happy match since Charles is Scorpio, another water sign like Diana. Theoretically these two should have swum along in blissful symbiosis for the duration. But the moment the sun signs are moved out of the way, a far more volatile and challenging picture emerges—a recipe for a marriage made in hell rather than heaven. Charles's sun at birth was at the particular point in Scorpio that enabled it to home right in to Diana's difficult moon-Venus-Uranus alignment. If you can imagine a three-legged chair waiting for the fourth to balance it, this is effectively what happens with the astrology. Charles became Diana's all-important fourth leg. In other words, he had the potential to balance her and make her whole—and vice versa. Yet human nature being what it is, he also had the power to throw her already rocky nature into complete disarray.

As I put it in 1981,

Although this configuration indicates that there are some incredibly powerful crosscurrents between them (which may result in blockbusting rows), the fact that Charles's sun forms this contact indicates there is a strong and compelling attraction between them . . . The karmic link cannot be ruled out here, nor can the manifestation of the control and frustration of energies. Perhaps Charles's innate self-control may give the appearance of abject coldness on occasion; he may feel compelled to pull Diana into line, which may crush her expansive and freedom-loving personality . . . Each of them will have to watch a tendency to blow hot and cold and "freeze" each other out when hurt. Both Scorpio and Cancer have a tendency to detach themselves from painful situations whilst internally brooding about them, so from time to time there will be marathon icy silences at Highgrove.

I also suspected that the sexual arena of the relationship would be its make-or-break point. In the chart of the relationship itself, Mars, the planet of physical drive and sexual motivation, was placed next to Neptune—a mysterious and elusive influence that gave two distinctly opposite prognoses. The first, that Diana and Charles would find an ecstatic level of sexual harmony—they may experience that rare sense of souls touching. And the second, that sexually they were a complete mismatch and that this would lead to the separate-beds syndrome fairly rapidly.

They are a charismatic couple, but the glamorous, high-gloss image the world has of them is, of course, an illusion. The danger of this illusion is that one or both people may be unable to come to terms with the everyday functioning of the relationship and therefore become disillusioned with the partner. On the positive side of Mars and Neptune, this could indicate a deep concern for humanitarian issues and much compassion and sensitivity displayed towards the world's suffering. This conjunction reflects a true missionary spirit and perhaps the existence of a high spiritual bond.

The Mars-Neptune conjunction does little to allay the suspicions that sexual problems will arise in the relationship. Neptune diffuses the energy (sexual and otherwise) of Mars, which can imply that the relationship may ultimately become platonic. And Saturn casts a rather austere shadow on their shared feelings, emotional and sexual.

In truth, there were so few good astrological contacts between these two in the sexual department of the relationship that it would have needed all that Neptune could throw at it in the way of soul contact and divine union to keep it afloat. Both Diana and Charles individually have charts that radiate sexuality. Consequently the likelihood that they would have to seek sexual love outside their relationship was extremely strong. I was to learn how very true this was five years later. But at the time of the wedding, perhaps the strongest concern I had about the marriage and its future was the respective ages of Charles and Diana.

The thirteen-year age gap was not in itself the main problem but the fact that at twenty, Diana had another decade to go before she would be fully formed as a woman, while Charles was already, at thirty-three, his own man. From an astrological point of view the twenty-ninth year of life is the demarcation point between youth and adulthood. It is at this time that Saturn returns to its original position in the natal horoscope, having taken twenty-nine years to orbit the sun. Until that time, we are experimenting with life and reflecting other people's views of who we are. We are not our own person. By our thirtieth year, we are meeting life on our own terms. We know some things work for us and others don't. We know what we want from existence and are ready to make long-term commitments.

I knew in my heart of hearts that Diana with this extraordinarily volatile and passionate chart would not cope well with a lifetime's marriage sentence hanging over her head. She was the sort who needed to experiment with her sexuality and her emotions before committing herself in the long term. I could see her becoming utterly bored with a man so completely set in his ways as Charles. By twenty-nine, she could have got much of this out of her system and be able to handle the constraints of marriage to a man, regardless of his age, and be able to meet a man considerably older with her own experience. As it was, the trapped butterfly was an image that leapt out of the astrology. In my book *Synastry: The Astrology of Relationships,* I had chosen my words carefully and suggested that women with such a pattern in their charts usually experienced "several romantic encounters in a lifetime." A little later on I used the phrase "break out of the marriage in order to seek new and more exciting horizons." This was juxtaposed by a comment about divorce for a future Queen of England being unthinkable. It was a polite way of saying that Diana's chart gave every indication she would find herself in the divorce courts.

It was extremely difficult for me to marry what I saw in her astrology to what I knew to be impossible in real terms. But I was haunted by the feeling that this marriage, with so much astrological tension in it, would eventually snap.

It took some five years for me to discover that my fears were indeed justified and that Diana and Charles, far from the united and happy image they presented to the world—especially on their glamorous royal tours—were deeply unhappy and desperately seeking a way out.

II

Tea, Sympathy, and Two Tylenol

❦

At one time I would have recoiled at the notion that fate was a powerful force in my life—or, indeed, anyone's life, come to that. But over the years, my experience as an astrologer and the extraordinary way my own life has unfolded has taught me otherwise. There are times when I know in every fibre of my being that I have been guided to be at a particular place at a particular time. From that point an elaborate fabric of events is woven that eventually makes a small piece of history. In some cases that history is relevant only to the few people directly involved. It has no place in the great scheme of things. But in some cases, a small piece of history has a much wider impact.

To begin the chain of events that led to my first meeting with the Princess of Wales, we must go back to 1981. And to yet another phone call one morning— from an unknown American woman requesting a written astrological analysis for a friend's birthday. At first I refused, since I was under pressure to finish a book. But eventually I was won over. There was some mystery over the identity of the woman whose chart I had been asked to interpret. I was given a pseudonym of Cathy Masters and told only that she had been married and had children.

I completed the analysis over a three-week period and dutifully sent it off. Two weeks later I received a grateful reply from Ms. Masters and assurances that she would contact me when she came to England in the spring. And she kept her word. It was when she phoned me that I was able to ask who she really was. Kathy du Ross came the answer. Unfortunately, having no familiarity with the American gossip columns and the American social scene, I still had absolutely no idea who she was. And it was only when I arrived at the country home of Henry Ford II a week or so later that I put two and two together. Kathy and Henry had been living together for several years after spending almost ten of them "underground" when he was still married to his second wife, Christina.

Kathy was to become a great friend, and although it was difficult not to be permanently in awe of Henry, he was always good company. He could be pugnacious and acerbic, but there was an impish quality about him. And his wry sense of humor was a joy. He was also endlessly tolerant of astrology and mysticism—Kathy's passions—which were the very antithesis of his pragmatic nature.

I will always carry with me the memory of the first time I met Henry. I had driven to this graceful Queen Anne mansion set in the wildly beautiful Oxfordshire countryside in my ancient Morris Minor. Feeling faintly embarrassed about arriving at the home of Ford itself in an old banger, I parked it under a mammoth conifer just outside the gates to the drive. When it came time for me to go, Henry insisted on seeing me personally to the car, and nothing I could say would deter him. He was somewhat perplexed and most amused when we began to walk out of the small garden, beyond the courtyard, past the kitchen garden, and eventually out of the grounds completely. And even more amused at the lengths to which I had gone to disguise my humble mode of transport. But worse was to come. The car refused to start, and it fell to Henry to give me a push-start down the hill.

It was the first of many visits to Turville over the years, although by the next one, I made sure I had a car that wouldn't need a kick-start. Even from a very famous foot.

It was in August of 1985 that I was asked to join the Fords for an impromptu dinner. Kathy had become a keen amateur photographer and, at the request of Koo Stark, had been invited to a photographic exhibition in London. It was there that she had been introduced to Gene Nocon, one of the greats in the photographic world. They had hit it off so well that Kathy had invited him and his wife, Liz, to dinner thinking we would make an interesting mix.

She was right. We all got on famously. Halfway through dinner, Gene asked me what I was currently working on, and I told him of my book that was to include twenty-four profiles of famous people. I mentioned that I was intending to interview all the celebrities with the exception of Prince Andrew, whose profile I had just finished.

Gene leaned across the table and said to Liz, "Penny's written something about Andrew in her book."

"Oh, he must see it. Can we have it, Penny? He'd be fascinated."

Gene, of course, was Andrew's photographic mentor. But I had no idea just how close the friendship was between the three of them. And while Gene gave Andrew the benefit of his photographic expertise, Liz was a valued confidante and immensely supportive during his affair with Koo—and later its demise.

The following day I sent off the manuscript to Liz and thought no more about it. One of the points I had mentioned in this profile was that Andrew had a "kingly" chart and that he was far more traditional and conservative—more typical of the royal firm—than Charles. Liz picked up on this immediately, backing up my intuition that Andrew was by far the favored son where taking on the mantle of the monarchy was concerned. Later she was to comment that Andrew had found the piece "intriguing" even though he had little interest in astrology.

The months passed. Liz and I met from time to time. Then, one evening in early January of 1986, she phoned. Would I do a chart for someone and look at it in connection with Andrew—and could it be done there and then? I agreed and wondered who the person was. At that time, my family was on a massive economy drive and our newspaper intake had been reduced to the *Times* and the *Sunday Times* only. Thus I had no idea whose name was beginning to dominate the gossip columns. More specifically, whose name was being romantically linked with Andrew.

I was given the time of birth as 9:30 A.M. in London on October 15, 1959. (This was later refined to 9:03 A.M.) At first glance there seemed relatively few significant connections between these two charts, but what did intrigue me was how closely this mystery female's horoscope linked to the rest of the royal family's charts.

I rang back an hour later and, after a short rundown of essential points with Liz, gave her my results: Yes, she did have a connection with Andrew. More important, Andrew was at the point in his life when he was astrologically primed to fall in love. Perfect timing rather than a perfect match. The phone was then handed over and Sarah Ferguson herself came on the line.

I can only describe this conversation as breathless

and taken at a gallop. Sarah, with her moon in feisty Aries, and I, with the sun in the same sign, were able to cover the essential ground in just less than the speed of sound. She was clearly desperately in love and desperately seeking assurances that she was right for Andrew. Not for the first time, my skills as a diplomat were called for.

It was obvious to a trained astrological eye that this was not going to be the match of the century—for reasons that I explain in Chapter VI—but when someone is in love, he or she is exceedingly vulnerable and liable to overreact to any comment that might imply the relationship would not lead to happy-ever-afterness. Also, and more important, love can override the most difficult astrological connections. So I encouraged her with my reasonings that anyone with such major planetary links to the royal family's charts was going to be more than an isolated ship passing in the night. Sarah was effusive with her thanks and asked if we could meet soon.

About two weeks later, Liz, Sarah, and myself all met in a restaurant in Notting Hill Gate—my choice, mainly because Sarah by that time was running the gauntlet of photographers and any of her known "haunts" were on continual media surveillance. During lunch Sarah mentioned that Diana would love to have her chart done, and would I do it? I said I would be delighted, but until I completed *Romancing the Stars,* I would have no time for any consultancy work.

The next time I was asked the same question was by Prince Andrew. We were at dinner at the Nocons'.

Andrew and Sarah had come from Windsor Castle, where Andrew had just asked the Queen's permission to marry Sarah. In effect we were the first people outside the royal family to know of their engagement. It was a stunning piece of news, and the atmosphere around the dinner table was electric and very bubbly indeed. During coffee, Andrew mentioned that his sister-in-law would love to have her chart done. For a moment I was confused and actually thought he was talking about Princess Anne. I expressed surprise, commenting that she seemed the last person who would be interested in astrology. A look of puzzlement came over Andrew's face, and I immediately realized my mistake. And for the second time I explained that I was under pressure to finish a book, but when I had completed it, I would be delighted to "do" Diana's chart.

Even in this relaxed and exceedingly happy atmosphere, Andrew could be daunting. And it was the second time that evening I definitely gained the impression that I had said the wrong thing. A little earlier, trying to grapple with the delicate balance between observing royal protocol and the art of easy conversation, I asked about the Queen and referred to her as "your mother."

"You mean, Her Majesty," he said with a reprimanding glower.

A matter of days after this dinner, the phone rang. And for the first time I heard Diana's distinctive voice at the other end of the line.

At first, we talked of Sarah and Andrew, and how she knew Sarah was "absolutely right" for Andrew and how well Sarah would fit in with the family, and how wonderful it would be to have a friend in the family. Eventually the conversation came to its essential point. Could I possibly do her chart?

"I'm so sorry," I replied, "I have absolutely no time for anything but finishing this wretched book. But I will see you the moment I have."

"I quite understand. When will the book be finished and what's it about?"

We talked around the book for a while, then she returned to the subject of her chart. She was fascinated about astrology, she said, and had always wanted "it" done. But now she had a reason. I assumed it was something to do with her wanting another baby and the hope that it might be a girl. But her voice broke and she faltered.

"You see, I just wanted to know if there was a light at the end of the tunnel . . ."

It was as if an ice cube had been traced down my spine. The pain in her voice was palpable.

"I'll come immediately," I said.

The following Thursday I made my way to Kensington Palace. And yet again the car problem reared its ugly head.

By now I was driving a seven-year-old Volkswagen Passatt—a little bruised and battered, but reliable. No, Penny, I thought, you cannot, simply cannot, drive into Kensington Palace to meet the Princess of

Wales in this. My credibility as one of Britain's leading astrologers—at least that's what my book jackets said—was in jeopardy. So I drove to the Royal Garden Hotel, parked in the underground car park, and walked up to the palace.

Like most people, I had no conception of what Kensington Palace was really like. My unconscious had somewhere retained the image of palaces as they are portrayed in fairy tales—all glistening and shimmering in splendor. But of course, Kensington Palace, or KP as it is more affectionately known, is much more like a huge country house. And even then it is split into separate apartments for various members of the royal family, including Princess Margaret and the Kents.

I arrived at the police box halfway up the drive and gave my name. I was checked against a list and a phone call was put through to the palace. I was then allowed to go ahead to the main drive. As I rounded the corner, Diana came out of the front door to greet me.

I had been told to curtsy and say, "How do you do, Your Royal Highness," but she waved the formality away and said, "Please call me Diana and don't bother to do that [the curtsy] again!"

Diana was wearing a straight skirt and a roll-neck sweater. She looked every bit as lovely in real life as she had in photographs and on film. I had also chosen to wear something casual—a rather unimpressive dress, in fact, mid-calf in length and khaki with a red collar. I had deliberately chosen not to buy anything new to mark the occasion because I wanted to feel at ease in every way I could. I wanted nothing to emphasize the fact that this was probably one of the most important moments of my life.

Diana led the way up the stairs to a small sitting room, and after my coat had been taken, I sat down at one end of a large pink sofa. She sat down beside me and, somewhat predictably, cut the ice by talking about Sarah and Andrew again. We waited until tea and some biscuits had been brought in before we began in earnest with the astrology.

I had two choices. Either I could let her tell her story, then spend the entire consultation dealing with the central issues, or I could adopt my normal course with a new client, which was to go over the basics of the chart, without any input from the person herself or himself, and ask for comments afterwards—a process that normally took about twenty minutes. This procedure served two purposes. First, it allowed me to "get into" the chart, and second, it permitted clients to get used to my style and to feel at ease with me.

I opted for the latter. A first consultation should be an unforgettable experience. For many people it is the first time anyone has plumbed their depths and seen their interior shadows; the first time their pain, their hopes, and their dreams have been really addressed. In some cases it can seem as though the very soul has been tapped and connected with. And at the end of the consultation, far from feeling at the mercy of fate, clients should sense that life is unfolding as it should —and with their participation.

I decided I would treat Diana in exactly the same way as I would any other client. If I was to continually defer to her royal standing, it would interfere with the balance of the relationship, which at that moment meant that I was in the position of authority! This is not to say that my role as an astrologer was a great power trip, but there was a need—indeed, as there always is—to take command of the situation.

I explained how I would be working with her, and she was eager to begin.

I began at the beginning—with her rising sign of Sagittarius. I described how this fiery and adventurous part of the horoscope represented her persona and acted as a doorway to her Self and all its component parts. This was the side of her, I explained, that she projected—the sunny, outgoing Diana. But this was a considerable contrast to her sensitive, moody, and caring side, which was reflected by her sun in the sign of Cancer. I pointed to Venus in Taurus and the placing of Neptune as the indicators of her love of dancing and her compassionate and spiritual side. I also mentioned that Mars in her chart was so close to Pluto that it gave a terrifically Scorpionic feel to the astrology. This was why Charles, as a sun Scorpio, was an ideal "choice" of a husband. I went on to say that Mars and Pluto were also linked to her early life, and this was an astrological reason her childhood had been so traumatic.

When I had finished, I asked how she had found it. "Fascinating . . . really me," she said.

Since I had finished my twenty-minute "intro" with the subject of her childhood, Diana picked up on this first.

Yes, her early life had indeed been awful. She talked about the constant loneliness she felt and the lack of attention—not in the sense that she was ignored and her material wants denied, but more that no one took the time to "really listen" and give her the deep affection she required. She went on at some length about the indignation she and her sisters (Jane and Sarah) and brother (Charles) felt when their father married Raine. This indignation was soon overridden by sheer hatred. Raine was the archetypal evil stepmother if not the prototype of the Wicked Witch of the West.

I had been laboring under the media myth that Diana was very close to her father during her childhood—Johnny Spencer had gained custody of the children after a bitter and acrimonious divorce from Diana's mother, Frances. But this was far from the truth. Diana found him distant and remote, and if he wasn't being unreachable, he was being angry and intolerant. Somewhere, not even very deep down, she knew he had driven her mother away, yet at the same time she felt utterly abandoned by Frances.

I was also to discover that Diana's relationship with her mother had been somewhat fictionalized by the media. There was no genuine closeness between them, even in her adult years. The childhood sense of no one being there for her, no one to really understand her and cater for her huge emotional needs, was an ever-open wound.

Her frank and honest comments now began to make the rough sketch of her early life as portrayed by the astrology into a recognizable structure. I had pointed the finger at Raine for fulfilling the promise in Diana's chart of the moon—the symbol of mother, childhood, and the feminine. And Diana's moon was in deep trouble. It revealed the lack of closeness and emotional connectedness with the mother and suggested that Diana's ambivalent feelings and experience of "mother" could create a breeding ground for emotional problems later. As it turned out, it was not just her stepmother who had proved unfit for the job of mothering, but her own mother, as well. However, I have to make it clear here that this was not necessarily a fault on Frances's part but how Diana, the child, *perceived* and *experienced* her mother.

So things were beginning to make more sense.

Diana also picked up on my mentioning her love of dance, and because I had been a dancer with the Royal Ballet Company in my earlier years, we talked at length about the discipline involved in ballet and how much we both couldn't resist dancing to the music, whether we were alone in a drawing room or in a proper studio.

But eventually we came to the nitty-gritty—the state of her marriage to Charles.

Now, of course, since the publication in 1992 of

various books on the Princess of Wales, the whole world knows how unhappy she was virtually from the outset. But on that day in early March 1986, it was a complete revelation. The extent of her despair was heartrending.

Quite the most moving remarks were those about the days surrounding the wedding. She had told me almost at once about Charles's affair with "a certain woman." (Diana did not mention who this person was during our first meeting but identified her the next consultation—see Chapter III.) She believed that Charles would drop this woman as soon as he was married. But not only did he continue to see her, according to Diana, he had been with this person on the eve of their wedding. In fact, Diana's very words were—and they are recorded clearly in my notes— "He spent the night before the wedding with this woman." Furthermore, on the day before they married, Charles told Diana categorically that he did not love her.

I have absolutely no idea if the facts support her statement of Charles spending his "stag night" with another woman. Charles certainly spent the earlier part of the evening of July 28, 1981, lighting the first of a chain of celebratory bonfires in Hyde Park. But, of course, he did not spend all night in the park. All I can say is this is precisely what Diana told me.

Thus, as she walked towards the altar, far from the radiant princess in a fairy tale, she was a nineteen-year-old choking back the pain of knowing the man she was about to exchange vows with—the love of her young life—did not reciprocate that love and was, indeed, in love with another woman.

"Halfway down the aisle I wanted to turn back."

In retrospect, this shows the enormous courage Diana is capable of summoning. And my heart went out to her utterly at that moment.

By her own admittance, Diana was very much in love with Charles when she married him. And even though he had told her point-blank that he was not in love with her, she believed that she could win him over when she was firmly ensconced as his wife.

But this was simply not to be.

Although the honeymoon had shown her that Charles could indeed respond to her love, by the time they were at Balmoral in August of 1981, that bright flame of hope had already begun to dwindle.

As her chart reveals, Diana is an exceedingly emotionally needy person. She requires constant assurances that she is loved. She needs to know that she is the epicenter of her loved one's life. His happiness must rest in her—as hers does in him. And any evidence to the contrary will send her into a spiral of rejection; feelings of abandonment experienced in her childhood rise to the surface and threaten her entire security system. Even quite legitimate absences on the loved one's part are interpreted as lack of love.

And so, in Balmoral, as Charles slipped back comfortably into the routine of the annual family break, pursuing many of his much-loved pastimes, most of them solitary, it seemed to Diana that he was rejecting her. Thus the emotional dynamics of their relationship began to take hold and the seeds of their future alienation were sown. The more Diana demanded of him emotionally and the more pressures she put upon him to be with her, the more distant and removed he became.

Had Diana been older and more experienced, she might have been able to comprehend that, by perpetuating this push-pull pattern, she was reducing the chances of Charles drawing nearer to her. As it was, she was ensuring that he would never fall in love with her. And while, with a little more time, she could have acquired the skill to deal with Charles, her pregnancy three months into the marriage, with all the attendant hormonal changes, made an already delicate situation critical.

Most men, and certainly most Englishmen, find emotions a gray area, but Charles, with his upbringing and his emotionally complex chart, freezes when the emotional temperature rises above "normal." According to Diana, there were almost daily incidents that reflected his lack of sympathy and understanding, and on some occasions, he had been cold to the point of abject cruelty. Diana asked me how I would feel if I had not seen my husband for over twenty-four hours, despite his being in the same building. And when, in desperation, I had knocked at his study door, it had been opened by his secretary, who informed me I would have to make an appointment!

"There I was in floods of tears, just needing him. And I'm told I have to book an appointment—with my own husband."

I could only identify, as indeed would any woman in a similar circumstance, with her sense of rejection. Diana's distress in reliving this incident and others was very real. There was no question in my mind at the time that Diana was not just living in an emotional vacuum with Charles, but the equivalent of a kind of hell.

According to Diana, she had reached the point at which she could no longer go on. She wanted out of the whole royal "setup." She asked me if she would find happiness with someone else—ever. And if so, how might that come about? She also asked me what kind of man was right for her astrologically.

By this point in the consultation, my perception of Diana was not that of a princess who needed to be humored but a young woman desperate to replace despair with hope—to find something that would give her a reason to go on. I had seen many clients in unhappy relationships, but none whose relationship mattered to the nation. Nevertheless I felt that this latter, albeit hugely important, factor had to be left out of the picture. I also knew that whatever else I did that afternoon, I had to leave her with a sense that she could cope, that there was hope and that leaving Charles at this juncture was not the answer.

As I looked at her chart, with all its difficult planetary transits that would take some years to clear, I felt that honesty—at least a bald statement—would be the worst policy. I told her that the short-term picture was by no means easy but that eventually she would find the happiness she craved. I also told her that it was early days to write off the marriage and that there were still ways she could find to make it work.

Clearly the fact that there was another woman in Charles's life made Diana's job of salvaging the marriage much more difficult. At that time, she did not disclose the name of the other woman, although I privately believed it to be Camilla Parker Bowles. I suggested to Diana that berating Charles for seeing another woman was pointless. The more Diana clung to him and made demands on him, the more she would drive him into the arms of his lover. I urged her to make a friend of her "opposition." In any extra-marital relationship, the betrayed wife or husband is the thorn in the lovers' side: They are united against a common "enemy." However, if the enemy becomes a friend, the relationship between the lovers is changed and a creeping sense of guilt starts to sour the union. After all, there's a certain amount of justification in betraying someone who is behaving like a harridan. It's not so easy when the harridan is sweet, acquiescent, and continually wielding an olive branch.

Diana could see the sense in offering the hand of friendship and thereby defusing the situation, and maintained she would "have a go."

"Fight fire with fire," I encouraged. "Don't be a victim."

Concerning her question about the astrological sign that was "right" for her in regard to a partner, I

pointed out that the sign governing the area of relationships in her chart was Gemini. Therefore, she
would gravitate to someone with a strong Mercurial or
Geminian theme in his chart. Somewhat ironically, I
was to discover later that her personal detective from
the royal protection squad, Sergeant Barry Mannakee,
was indeed a Gemini.

During the consultation I placed great emphasis on
the fact that she was not doomed to remain forever in
a loveless marriage, trapped, like a butterfly, in the
prison of the royal family. I chose my words carefully
and said, "You will be allowed out one day." What I
meant was that fate would find a way to release her
from the situation. It was only in 1992, when I read
Andrew Morton's book, that I realized Diana had
taken my statement to imply that the family would
allow her out.

*Diana admitted to Penny that she couldn't bear
the system. "One day you will be allowed out as
opposed to divorcing," Penny told her, confirming
Diana's existing opinion that she would never
become Queen.*

In order to enable Diana to understand the dynamics of her relationship with Charles and the routes to
resolving certain patterns, I placed three charts on the
table in front of us: hers and Charles's and a third—
the chart of the relationship itself. I showed her the
way the charts connected and the reasons why hers
and Charles's destinies were so interlinked. Pointing

to the configuration I describe in Chapter I as a "three-legged chair," I explained that this was the reason they were so powerfully drawn together, yet also the factor that could render them oceans apart. I encouraged Diana to see how her need for love was the very factor that drove Charles away. And that by restraining her demands—even if she had to act that way at first—he would become more accessible to her.

I also felt that her excessive need to be loved would be less pressing if she had another outlet—another passion, if you like. So I suggested that one way of transmuting emotional pain was to relate to other people's suffering. In this way one's pain became a thing of beauty, not a continual burden. I showed her that the elevated position of Neptune in her chart indicated she had a strong spirituality and that this would not only guide her through her darkest hours but could be positively accessed to help others.

I could not be sure at the time whether any of these suggestions would be acted upon, but I did notice that she lost her aura of desperation and she seemed more centered altogether.

I had also mentioned to Diana that right from childhood she may have experienced a strong sense of her own destiny.

"I knew very early on in my life that I was born to do something special. And I knew I was destined to marry a great man. Somewhere along the way I began to know that man was Charles."

According to Diana, her father would also tell her when she was little that he knew she was destined for great things. And while every father may believe this of every daughter, in Johnny Spencer's case he was, despite his chauvinistic and earthy temperament, not unfamiliar with things of the spirit. (Barbara Cartland, his mother-in-law, told me that in her opinion, one of the principal reasons Lord Spencer recovered from his near-fatal stroke—if not the main reason—was the power of prayer.) It was while we were talking about destiny that Diana asked me about Charles. I had long held a belief that Charles might well not make it to the throne, so I beat around the bush for a while so as not to upset her. Suddenly, turning to a photograph of Charles, she said, "It's all right. I've always known he'll never be King. And I'll never be Queen." It was a stunning remark to make. And because it came out of the moment—a moment when we were both very open in a psychic sense—there was an absolute feel of truth about it. It is a moment I will never forget.

Somehow, four hours had passed. We had covered an enormous amount of ground and, not surprisingly, I was beginning to flag. I also had a thumping headache. Diana sweetly went and got me two painkillers herself, apologizing for having worked me so hard. As if entirely on cue, William and Harry came bounding in and, like any young boys, immediately raided the biscuit plate. Then, after a brief exchange of formalities, they disappeared as quickly as they had arrived. It formed a natural end to our meeting.

Diana thanked me for "everything," and I told her to ring me any time she felt the need. The intimacy of the consultation had created an affectionate bond between us and we bade each other a warm good-bye. I don't even remember walking past the police box.

Later that evening I was phoned by Sarah. She gave me the message that Prince Charles was immensely grateful for what I had done. I was slightly bemused because I believed he had no idea I had seen Diana. In conversation with Liz Nocon six days later she informed me that Diana was at crisis point when I had "gone in." Apparently "her bags were packed." Thankfully no one had told me this beforehand. The pressure of knowing that so much rested on my reversing the situation might well have interfered with my ability to resolve it.

A job well done, I hoped. But this was not the end, only the beginning.

III

A Question
of Divorce

⌘

One of the questions I was repeatedly asked in the
wake of the revelations that Diana had consulted an
astrologer was how many times I had seen her;
furthermore, could I produce evidence that I had? As
I explain later, in the spring of 1993 my job as *Today*
newspaper's astrologer was placed on the line unless I
could prove that my association with the Princess of
Wales was genuine. In the event, I declined to reveal
any evidence whatsoever. But this issue of proof
regarding a client-astrologer relationship brought up
an interesting point. By great irony, it revealed that of
all my clients, the one of whom I had most proof was
Diana.

An astrological counselor, like any psychotherapist
or psychologist, will see clients on a regular basis until

the client has worked through the relevant issues and processed them. And that can take weeks, months— even years. But an astrologer who is seeing a client for purely astrological guidance may never see that client more than once. In fact, if he or she is doing the job well, there is no need for constant updates. The majority of my clients have fallen into this latter category. Not, I hasten to add, because I'm so hopeless at my job no one ever wants to come back, but because the consultation is comprehensive. Clearly there are times when clients are facing huge life changes and need detailed advice, encouragement, and guidance—over the phone or by consultation—until they have safely negotiated their crises. And one or two people require very precise information on a day-to-day level for business purposes. But a typical client sees me once, then returns six months to a year later. In between I have no contact with them whatsoever. Not a letter of thanks. Not a phone call. Not even a Christmas card. And many clients do not pay by check. So, in terms of proof, there would only be my diary entries of their appointments, their details on my computer, and my handwritten notes.

Diana was the exception to the rule. And for the six years between March of 1986 and March of 1992 a dialogue was maintained, largely over the phone and through correspondence. And a relationship of mutual trust and affection was built up.

The Sunday following my first visit to Kensington Palace, Diana phoned to thank me and to say that she felt much stronger and more able to cope than she had for some time. Three days later she phoned again to let me know that she had asked Barbara Cartland, on my behalf, if she would agree to an interview for the book I was writing. Miss Cartland, she informed me, was only too delighted to consent.

The call also provided another opportunity for Diana to be reassured that even though her life wasn't going to turn the corner overnight, it could and would change. She would eventually find happiness.

Diana had made a profound impression upon me when I met her. I found her warm, self-deprecating, very open, and very vulnerable. She listened well, asked intelligent questions, and was overridingly anxious that her marriage to Charles could be turned into a happy-ever-after story. However, I could see from her chart that she was in for an extremely difficult decade—one when she would need all the help and good advice available.

But in the spring of 1986 I had my own set of challenges, or rather deadlines, to meet. And Sarah Ferguson was the more pressing concern and certainly the one with whom I had most contact (see Chapter VI). It wasn't until after Sarah's wedding to Prince Andrew that Diana became my sole concern within Palace walls.

In August of that year, Diana appeared in one of my dreams looking distressed, if not in utter despair. The dream had such a profound effect on me, I thought I ought to contact her. Diana had given me her direct number at Kensington Palace, but I chose instead to write.

Although, in the main, the content of the letter was light and chatty, my real intent was to encourage her to keep going—regardless.

> *When we spoke in March I think I mentioned that there were some indications in your chart that the clash you felt between duties, responsibilities, and pressures generally as opposed to the fresh air and freedom you require would continue for some time and that you had to grin and bear it. It occurred to me that from this August and into October you might feel particularly unsettled and, with the pressure from all corners, you may feel even more "trapped" by circumstances. All I can do is urge you to hang on and not to do anything you may regret later. Life will not always be like this. It will change without your giving it any extra help!*

Diana telephoned me on the afternoon of the sixth, thanking me for the letter and saying that she had wanted to ring many times but thought I might consider her "a bit cranky." She phoned again in the evening and we spoke at length about the continuing unhappiness she felt and the best way to cope with Charles's lack of affection and his inability to relate to her plight. What was making her distress even more acute was the daunting prospect of the family holiday at Balmoral. She joked about it, but behind the banter was the clear dread of the annual ordeal. In the event, my advice and encouragement proved to no avail. And all her best intentions to "stick with it" collapsed under the weight of her sense of hopelessness and isolation. On October 12, some two months later, Liz Nocon was to inform me that, after returning from Balmoral, Diana had left Charles. But, as Andrew had gone on to confide to her, she had been "brought back pretty quickly." So, while six months earlier, I had been able to inspire in her the strength and purpose to stay, under the weight of a fresh barrage of unhappiness she had again reached the point of flee rather than fight.

An astrologer can give someone the best advice in the world, but it's always up to the individual to choose whether or not to follow it. And while this may seem like a criticism of Diana, the intent is to reveal the sovereignty of free will and also how truly desperate Diana felt. But, of course, the bolt served an important purpose in that it showed her that such an action was in any event to no avail. Liz, of course, was extremely close to both Andrew and Sarah at this time, and the topic of conversation would often center on the Waleses. Liz added that Sarah and Andrew were beginning to share the royal family's view that Diana was going ever so slightly mad. It was said jokingly, of course, but nonetheless it was apparent that Diana was experiencing considerable difficulty in maintaining an even keel—or at least giving the impression of being a well-balanced individual. I never questioned Diana as to the veracity of Liz's comment on her post-Balmoral defection, but by the time I next saw her, it was clear the situation between her and Charles, far from improving, had sunk way below any acceptable watermark.

Telephone calls—always her initiative—came from time to time, but it wasn't until March 10, 1987, that we met again face-to-face. I was invited to lunch at Kensington Palace at 12:30 P.M.

This time I had more courage and drove brazenly up to the palace in the Passat. Once past the police box, I parked, feigning nonchalance, a little way from the main door.

Sadly, my notes on this consultation have mysteriously disappeared and I have only a slight recollection of what we discussed. I remember the lunch vividly, however: poached chicken with baked potatoes and salad. I declined dessert and opted for cheese.

Having said that my notes written up after our meeting are no longer in my possession, I do still retain those I made beforehand—in other words, the points I wanted to cover—and those are quite revealing.

Rather like a doctor who can turn to his patients' notes to establish what he prescribed for a set of symptoms, an astrologer is able to refer to the major contacts of the transiting and progressed planets to determine what would be under discussion. In Diana's case, in the spring of 1987, Neptune—a planet of mystery and the divine on the one hand, and gross deception, chaos, and unreality on the other— was in a highly prominent position: floating between the sun and Mercury in the area of relationships. Added to this, Saturn—a planet renowned for unremitting hardship and struggle—was overshadowing the Ascendant and therefore the relationship axis. Consequently, her chart was a recipe for disappointment, suffering, frustration, and betrayal. A theme that had been around for some considerable time and would continue unabated through most of 1988 and 1989. And although the main topic of our conversation would have been the relationship between her and Charles and the betrayal and suffering she was experiencing at his hands, I knew there would be other situations and other people who would almost certainly fulfill the astrological criteria.

I do remember saying during the consultation—and more than once in order to drive the point well and truly home—that Diana should be careful whom she trusted. Even her closest friends and apparently loyal supporters should not be placed above suspicion. As it happened, I knew full well that Sarah was being less of a friend to the Princess of Wales than Diana believed. Liz Nocon had voiced her concern to me over Sarah's seemingly inappropriate behavior regarding Diana. Apparently, not only was Sarah making the most of her position as the Queen's favorite daughter-in-law by cozily chatting to her about Diana's deeds and misdeeds and undermining her in the process, but she was peeking at Diana's mail in order to discover who was writing to her. Certain names were then casually dropped into her conversations with Prince Charles—a ploy that would add fuel to any of Charles's misgivings about Diana's associations and her overall stability.

I decided against directing her attentions to Sarah because such a move might well have been interpreted as "mixing it," and I firmly believe in allowing people to dig their own graves. I knew eventually Diana would discover such a truth for herself. And given the philosophy that life is the most experienced teacher of all, maybe Diana needed to learn the hard way. In retrospect perhaps it was a lesson she learned rather too well.

Sarah's star was in the ascendancy in 1987 and the media was showing signs of falling seriously in love with her—probably at the expense of Diana. And Sarah, given her fundamental insecurity and need to be loved, was entirely capable of exploiting the situation. And for the first eighteen months of her marriage to Andrew—effectively up to the debacle of BBC TV's *It's a Royal Knockout*—Sarah occupied a prominent place in Charles's affections. And quite a large part of that closeness was gained through her betrayal of Diana's trust. Charles even gave Sarah a necklace worth thousands of pounds for her birthday present the year she married Andrew.

By great irony, Diana was becoming closer to and more reliant on Sarah by the day. The situation was not exactly discouraged by the fact that she was continually being berated—particularly by Charles—for not being more like Sarah.

It took Diana until the summer of 1989 to discover the extent of Sarah's disloyalty.

But I still consider I took the right decision in not revealing any "insider information" in 1987. Not simply because it would have been somewhat unprofessional to mix gossip with sound astrological judgment but because it could have been untrue. However, it was difficult not to believe Liz Nocon at the time, since she had only the best of motives for telling me in the first place—to enable me to alert Diana. And time, of course, did prove Liz right.

Exactly as upon my first meeting with Diana, the consultation took place in the small sitting room on the first floor. And although I have only a scant recall of our dialogue on that occasion, I do remember feeling very close to her. Just before I left that afternoon, Diana disappeared for a moment and returned with a small pink package. At her bidding I opened it and inside was a tiny silver pillbox with two little bees on it.

"For your painkillers!" She smiled.

She had remembered having to give me some painkillers on our first meeting. It was a typically sweet and thoughtful gesture. I treasure the gift to this day.

And although I may not remember word for word what was discussed on our second meeting, I have a perfect recall of going straight to Harvey Nichols afterwards and buying an expensive outfit to mark the occasion—and I still have that blue suit to this day.

The year 1987 was not a good one for Diana. She appeared to be losing in the popularity stakes against Sarah. Indeed, her attempts to win Charles's approval by being more like Sarah seriously backfired. While the initial jolly jape before Sarah's wedding—dressing up as policewomen and storming a London nightclub—had been taken in good faith by the press, the umbrella-poking incident at Ascot in 1987 close on the heels of Diana's juvenile behavior at a Sandhurst passing-out ceremony created an outcry.

Andrew Morton's comment in the *Star* newspaper of April 27, 1987, is typical of the thoughts circulating in the press at the time.

> *Gone are the demure days when the main discussion among royal photographers was if the Princess was going to smile during a royal engagement. Now she giggles, smirks, and grins like a sixth former* [an adolescent] *on her first date. Her simpering style went down very badly when she reviewed the officer cadets at Sandhurst . . . At this solemn and sober occasion she treated the whole affair as a big joke. "Not the actions of a future Queen," one Sandhurst officer sadly remarked . . . Charles himself has publicly rebuked her more girlish behavior on the ski slopes . . . but he could do little about her mild flirtation with the President of Portugal when she jokingly twanged his braces on two official engagements. And even her advisors were powerless when she insisted on meeting reformed drug addict Boy George . . . Aristocrats within the royal circle now feel the Princess is behaving less like*

a potential Queen and more like a starstruck teenybopper.

On top of the press criticism Diana faced personally, there were rumblings of concern over the state of the marriage. News that they had separate bedrooms led to a flurry of articles debating the implications of sleeping alone. Anthony Holden was among several writers to make mincemeat of the notion that there was any trouble in the Waleses' marriage.

Can it really be true, as one Sunday paper recently suggested, that they have separate bedrooms? The answer is that this is a traditional royal practice. The Queen and Prince Philip have had separate bedrooms since their marriage . . . Separate bedrooms does not necessarily mean sleeping separately . . . The point is that a royal marriage cannot be conducted like those of ordinary mortals. It must be lived among an arduous routine of engagements which often have the couple heading in separate directions. Occasionally this week, it leads to fevered press innuendo. Why have they spent so much time apart this year? She returned early from the ski slopes . . . and now he has gone off alone for a week's painting in Italy. But spending time apart, so they can each "do their own thing"—and sharing out the time spent with the children can be the sign as much of a healthy and mature marriage as one heading into trouble. In the case of Charles

*and Diana . . . I believe the happier explanation
to be the true one . . . Unlike most superstar
couples, they know that there can never be any
question of separation or divorce. As the future
Supreme Governor of the Church of England,
Prince Charles must learn to live with his marriage, whatever ups and downs it may undergo.*
(*Today* newspaper, May 3, 1987)

The sort of well-informed comment that makes it
clear why a prophet is not recognized in his own
country . . .

After our March meeting, Diana and I spoke on the
telephone from time to time. She made an effort to be
chirpy but would confess to "things being a bit bleak."
According to my diary notes, on the day of her
birthday we had discussed the possibility that her
phone was tapped . . . October of 1987 is memorable
for many reasons. The city will remember it for Black
Monday—the day the stock market collapsed—and
the rest of the country for the first hurricane to hit
England in three hundred years. I remember that
October because my wedding anniversary weekend
was blown apart by the hundred-mile-per-hour gale.
And also because this autumn month marked my
third visit to Kensington Palace.

Earlier that year, my family and I had moved to a
remote and densely forested part of Hampshire. It
was, of course, delightful in the summer, but when the
hurricane struck it was truly a nightmare on Elm
Street—or Oak Lane, to be more precise. Our small

community was virtually the last pocket of humanity to have its electricity and water reconnected. It took ten days. We fared a little better with the telephone, which was put back on within the week. Almost the first person to phone was Diana.

I had half expected her to be in contact. The night before I had had a dream in which we were sitting together talking about our children. There were several other people milling about, and Diana was being gracious and cheerful. When I mentioned how well she was looking, her expression completely changed. And looking at me intently, she pressed my hand. The touch was so real, I awoke immediately. And I knew something was wrong.

The day before I was due to see her, I spent some considerable time going over her chart. And as the afternoon light gave way to dusk, what had started out as a simple enough list of transits and progressions had become an extraordinary spectre of Plutonic upheaval within the royal family.

Almost every astrologer will be familiar with the feeling of "getting into a chart." It's as though several gear changes have to be negotiated in order to move from first gear to top. Put another way, a series of shifts of perception is necessary to move from normal, everyday consciousness to an acute level of clarity.

I had begun by looking at Diana's chart for the period between October of 1987 and October of 1988. I then compared Charles's chart for the same period. I will return to the astrological facts of the piece shortly, but suffice to say, there was enough material to make me believe that something quite extraordinary was set to take place. But it didn't begin with 1987 and end with 1988: On through 1989, 1990, and into the mid 1990s I could see one difficult astrological passage leading into another. I was so fascinated that I went on to look at the Queen's chart and the rest of the leading royals, including Andrew and Sarah.

The key pieces on the astrological chessboard were Uranus, Neptune, Saturn, and Pluto. Saturn and the three outer planets are synonymous with huge change —the sort of change that is thrust upon people, not the sort that is gently brought into being. At the time I was to see Diana, Saturn was close to the most personal angle of the chart—the Ascendant— therefore, she was feeling the burden of unhappiness most acutely and feeling unequipped to deal with it. Saturn was to enter the sign of Capricorn in 1988 and, on its way to a rendezvous with its original position at birth—the Saturn Return—in January 1991, would oppose Mercury (the ruler of the zone of relationships) and the sun—the vital force of the chart. Whatever limitations Saturn sought to exert, throughout 1989 and 1990 Uranus would follow to create instability and emotional havoc. And, of course, our old friend duplicitous Neptune would be hard at work eroding trust and confidence at the same time.

If Diana was hard-pressed by the planets, Charles was positively on his knees. By far the most concerning transit was that of Uranus and Saturn. Since these two planets exert entirely opposite effects—the former releasing, the latter containing—an individual would feel as though he had one foot pressed hard down on the accelerator of his life, yet with the hand brake on at the same time. By the time this duo reached the opposition to Uranus at birth, the pressure would be akin to a huge volcano erupting with no escape hatch. And this was set to take place in February of 1988.

But all this seemed only a prelude to what was to come in 1992 with the arrival of Pluto at the key degree of twenty-two Scorpio. Pluto is known as the Great Transformer of the planets. I also call him the Great Fertilizer because his kind of influence acts like good manure on the garden. It may not smell very nice, but my goodness, it creates wonderful blooms. Pluto is great growth material. This degree area of twenty-two of the fixed signs (Scorpio, Taurus, Aquarius, and Leo) was already familiar to me because it is exactly the point of the zodiac at which Charles's sun rests. It is also the degree of the Queen's Mars, Jupiter, Neptune, and close to her Midheaven and Saturn. The Queen mother's moon is at this point, as is Prince Philip's moon. Not to mention Prince William's Venus, Prince Harry's moon, The Duke of York's moon, and the Duchess's Ascendant.

To be accurate, it wasn't the first foreboding I had experienced in regard to what might happen in the years to come to the royal family. In July of 1987 I had written an article entitled "Royalty: Red Alert." In the space of two thousand words or so I had discussed the possibility that Charles may not make it to the throne. And the reason? His divorce from the Princess of

Wales. I suggested that, were this scenario to take place in the early 1990s, Andrew might well take over as Regent until William was old enough to carry out Charles's official duties. Yet I also made the point that Sarah and Andrew looked unlikely to remain wedded together till death did them part. So a constitutional crisis could be brought about—almost by default.

Before I offered the article for publication, I sent Diana a draft, anticipating a rather strong reaction and a suggestion that it must never see the light of day. But she had been intrigued and wanted no alteration, nor to stand in the way of its publication. In the event, it was far too astrological for anyone to publish, but eventually "Royalty: Red Alert" became the basis for the profile of Prince Charles in *Romancing the Stars* that came out the following year.

Although, through the medium of an unpublished article, I had aired with Diana the possibility of divorce, it was impossible to gauge her real reaction to the prospect. Her cavalier attitude to what had been presented as conjecture might turn to hostility in the harsh light of a serious discussion. So, the night before I went to see her, I talked through my findings and presentiments with my husband, Simon. He supported me in my view that the potential for divorce should be downplayed at this stage because (a) it might set all the alarm bells going and precipitate another marital crisis and (b) the major events were still some ways off, allowing plenty of time to nurse the situation along while, at the same time, preparing the ground for separate lives.

But, as usual, Diana was way ahead of me. Or at least, entirely open to the notion that she and Charles were not destined to become the Victoria and Albert of the twenty-first century.

My arrival at Kensington Palace was somewhat different from the other visits. I arrived at the police box at eleven in the morning of October 29 and, after a furtive phone call, was ushered in through the "back door." As I entered the kitchen, Diana came rushing down the stairs apologizing profusely for such an oversight. It could not have mattered less. But she went to great pains to assure me that no slight had been intended.

Shortly after we had seated ourselves, coffee arrived. And, after a few pleasantries, I began to talk about her chart. I already knew from her phone call that she had reached yet another crisis of hopelessness.

Diana was always reluctant to reveal too much too soon. In this way she was typical of many people who need to feel very reassured before they open their hearts. One of the ways of encouraging that reassurance is to allow the astrology to speak for them. In other words, I would discuss what the current trends were likely to produce in the way of feelings and events, and because the client would identify with what was said, an open and intimate forum would be created. I suggested the growing chorus of concern in the press about the state of the marriage was forcing the issue between her and Charles. And she agreed. I then asked if their unhappiness had been discussed with the rest of the family. Diana said that it hadn't and commented that the family were behaving "like ostriches." It was apparent that the Queen was keeping her distance, and it was of some concern to Charles that since her return from Canada—some five days before—Her Majesty hadn't even been in touch on the phone. This, in addition to press speculation over the state of their marriage reaching fever pitch.

I put it to Diana that surely she and Charles could manage to live separate lives discreetly. Diana nodded in agreement and went on to say that she and Charles had thought the perfect solution was for him to base himself at Highgrove and for her to remain at Kensington Palace. "But the press won't have it." As Diana then saw it, the media was "hungry for blood and determined to separate us for good and proper."

I then suggested their putting on a united front. Lots of hand-holding and affectionate pecks in public. At this Diana guffawed, "Oh God, not like the Reagans—too terrible."

Rather more seriously, she added that after their visit to flood-damaged Wales in the aftermath of the hurricane, Charles had refused point-blank to spend the night with her in London. He was unprepared to make a gesture "just to put things right in the eyes of the world." She went on to say that Charles loathed his official duties. And sometimes he would be in such a trough of depression over what he perceived as a hopeless situation and a rudderless existence, Diana would almost have to push him out of the door. In my notes, I have made the comment "It is clear they are in no way prepared to try to bluff it out. I think they'll have to rethink this, actually."

According to Diana, she and Charles had reached a comparatively civilized "space." There had been an abatement in hostilities through a mutual recognition that they were both utterly miserable and both wanted "out." "We're completely incompatible. And there's nothing we can do. If we were anyone else, we'd be in the divorce courts by now!" Diana went on to say Sarah had been "wonderful" and had been trying to help by sitting them both down and allowing them to talk things through. The Spencers had also been extremely supportive—at least once they had overcome their initial shock. Apparently they had been completely ignorant of the increasing divide over the five years and had only been told in late '86 (presumably at the time of Diana's alleged bolt from Kensington Palace).

We returned over some old ground, too. Diana maintained that her arranged marriage was a romance created purely by the media. And she reiterated the account of Charles telling her the day before the wedding that he did not love her.

At this point the proverbial floodgates opened and her outrage at Charles's continuing relationship with another woman poured out. "He'll always love this other woman. He has for ten years . . . and she's unhappily married, too." I asked her if she meant Camilla Parker Bowles. She nodded.

This sharp change in mood from calm acceptance

of the status quo with Charles to the sudden upsurge of feeling about his betrayal was understandable. But it displayed what a knife edge she was living on.

I sympathized with her sense of betrayal, and reassured her that anyone would feel the same unless she were as insensitive as a brick. But, I urged, what would make her situation a whole lot better was doing something actively to change it. A sense of hopelessness could only lead to a spiral of negativity and despair. Since she had already brought up the subject of divorce, I tentatively raised it again. We discussed the fact that if she and Charles headed in that direction, it would be completely "unknown territory." There was no room for divorce in the Constitution. But it was clear that divorce had been mentioned between the two of them. Furthermore, Charles had given Diana his solemn assurance that she would not have to go away in disgrace. She would still be able to maintain a high profile. I added that, although he might wish her to sustain such privileges, it might not work out quite that way.

Clearly it was out of the question for Diana or Charles to approach a lawyer and calmly ask the best way to go about divorcing each other. So perhaps sounding out the family on the matter was the best course of action. I inquired who might be the most sympathetic of the "old guard" to their plight, and she opined Princess Margaret. By the time we were discussing the various tactics she and Charles might adopt, she was visibly less despairing. From a hunched position at the corner of the sofa, she became upright and animated. I explained that the worst sensation in the world was to feel trapped in a situation, to be a passive victim of fate. Once anyone is actively engaged in an escape plan, the situation becomes dynamic. Things move. Even mountains.

It was an extremely positive note upon which to end. And, as on previous occasions, she accompanied me out to the drive and thanked me profusely. Four days later, the most beautiful bunch of flowers arrived with a short note. "A million heartfelt thanks for your kindness . . ."

In retrospect, all sorts of issues are raised by what I was told then and what subsequently transpired. First, that both Diana and Charles had been entirely open to the possibility of divorce as far back as 1987. Second, that their relationship veered between relentless hostility, laced with outbursts of jealousy and anger on Diana's part, and periods of clarity and calm generated by the acceptance of their common fate. Therefore, contrary to the prevailing view that Charles and Diana had no meeting place at all in their marriage, the one factor that united them was their mutual quest to lead separate and therefore happier and more fulfilling lives.

Also, in retrospect, there were clear discrepancies in Diana's view of her marriage. On the first occasion I saw her, her desperation over her unrequited love for Charles and the devastation she felt on the eve of her wedding at his categorical denial of any love for her gave me the clear understanding that she married Charles for love. Love was paramount and she believed she would win his heart. Eventually. To her, the romance was real. Yet in October of 1987 she was to state unequivocally that the marriage was arranged and certainly heavily engineered by her grandmother, Lady Fermoy, and Queen Elizabeth, the Queen Mother—the implication being that there was no romance and, given a choice, she would not have entered into the marriage. Of course, that it was an arranged marriage would not preclude the fact that she married for love, even if he had not. And then, time does alter our perception of why we do the things we do . . . But clearly the journey Diana had made between the time I first saw her in March 1986 and October of 1987 was considerable.

In the beginning, Charles had the upper psychological hand, but by late 1987 the balance of power had shifted. To return to the astrological side of things, Diana, as a Cancerian, operates primarily through her emotions and instincts. When she is hurt she has two routes available: to go into her shell, sulk, and wait to be tenderly coerced out; or to strike back using her full emotional arsenal. Since Charles could not be moved by her because he was not in love with her, Diana was reduced to ever more excessive ways to gain a reaction from him. Eventually a combination of sheer exhaustion and common sense enabled her to round an important corner. Diana's brilliant career as Princess Superstar had clearly eclipsed Charles's as Prince Charming-and-Earnest by the early 1980s. But no matter how she enjoyed her success, the failure to have Charles wholly to herself—to have him open his heart to her—overrode any satisfaction she may have gained from her exalted professional status. Only when her success in her public role gave her back the power she had lost in the relationship did she begin to wield the whip in her marriage. As the realization dawned upon Charles that he was doomed forever to walk in his wife's formidable shadow, he began to see the end of the marriage as the perfect solution to all sorts of ills.

With power regained, Diana began to take on the role of parent in the relationship—a point exemplified by her insistence that the two of them put on a united front in the Wales episode. And Charles, adopting the role of the truculent child, refused to cooperate. As she became more in control, Charles not only increasingly shut her out but, as an act of retaliation, made an unconscious decision to self-destruct. Since he appeared to have got into a battle he clearly could not win, he began to question whether the battle was worth it. Would he ever clasp the reins of power, and even if he did, did he want them, anyway? All the turmoil provoked by the constant questioning of his true purpose (which had raged within him since he was thirty) was exacerbated by Diana's presence at his side. Instead of her being a foil for his dashing role, he was fast becoming his wife's sidekick. His path to the throne was not just being shared, but usurped. So, like a small boy, he decided he didn't want it.

I have to confess that this concept of Charles stamping his foot and turning his back on the throne is overblown. But there is no doubt that in the mid 1980s he came to the unbearably depressing realization that not only was his role as King-in-waiting undefined and deeply unfulfilling, but the likelihood of his claiming his Kingly destiny was becoming more remote by the day. And although I am sure he made no conscious decision to give up all hope of the throne, unconsciously he was deeply ambiguous about it. Certainly, if Diana was being truthful about his reluctance to go out and "do his job," Charles's loathing of public duties must have clashed violently with his lifelong programming for such responsibilities. And that kind of split would surely have played havoc in his unconscious. Had Diana not eclipsed him so totally, however, I am sure there would have been no reluctance on Charles's part to attend any and every official duty. As it was, by 1987 the combination of his unhappy marriage and his apparent uselessness drove him ever more inward. And around the time I saw Diana in the spring, he embarked on a four-day sojourn in the Kalahari Desert with his mystic mentor, Sir Laurens Van der Post.

Whatever signs Charles had shown before of his leaning toward all things green and mystical, his journey to the Kalahari made it clear that his search for spiritual sustenance was in dead earnest. In a world that failed him on so many levels, the search for an inner peace, a communion with his soul, was the one meaningful quest. Charles no doubt discovered an embarrassment of spiritual riches in the desert with the remarkable guide Sir Laurens to lead him.

But what he was able to bring back with him in the sense of an enlightened way of dealing with his real-life problems is questionable.

It seemed immensely sad to me at the time, and just as poignant now, that two people with so much potential in spiritual terms should find themselves so polarized and so desperately unable to help themselves individually or each other. What a cosmic irony that destiny had brought two such extraordinary and potentially enlightened people together—a royal couple with all the right raw ingredients to rule in a New Golden Age—who could not live as man and wife. Of course, there was always hope, always free will. But by early 1988, any hope of a reversal of the marital ice age was crushed on the ski slopes of Klosters.

IV

A Chilling Prospect

＊

In the early afternoon of March 10, 1988, a small group was skiing a piste near the notoriously difficult Wang run at Klosters. During the previous two weeks there had been exceedingly heavy snowfalls, which built up an increasingly unstable base, creating perfect avalanche conditions. It only required a slight movement from a skier or a shaft of sunshine on a slope to destabilize the fragile carpet of snow. At approximately 2:45 P.M., something did just that. Two of the party were swept under by the force of the avalanche; the rest were fortunate to be in a position to take evasive action.

According to Diana, there had been a strange and eerie atmosphere to the day right from the outset. She was nursing a heavy cold, and Sarah had had a nasty tumble down the Drostobel run before lunch. So the two women were together in Diana's room when the first rumblings of a disaster were heard.

It was the voice of Philip Mackie, Charles's press secretary, that cut into the afternoon warmth like a sliver of ice.

"There's been an accident . . ."

As Diana was to tell me later, she knew instantly that Charles had been involved. But at that time neither Philip nor anyone else was aware whether Charles was alive or dead.

"It was the most awful, awful time. We knew someone had been killed, and for about half an hour, we feared it was Charles."

Whatever anger Diana had felt for Charles, and however alienated she was from him, during that anguished wait she prayed and prayed for his life. When Charles finally came through the door, she rushed down to him and threw her arms about his neck.

"He just pushed me aside, Penny . . . He didn't want to know . . ."

In retrospect, it is clear that Charles was in such a state of grief and shock that he wanted nothing more than to be absolutely alone. It was his way of dealing with the enormity of what he had been through and the guilt and responsibility he felt for the death of his friend, Major Hugh Lindsay. But to Diana it was the final nail in the coffin of hope.

Back in England, some days after the funeral of

Major Lindsay, Diana spent three quarters of an hour on the phone to me describing her emotions on the day of the fatal accident. To her, it was a turning point. She felt that if Charles had fallen into her arms when he walked into the chalet—had come to her in his hour of need—their relationship would have been turned round completely. As it was, not even such a powerfully transformative event as a brush with death could bridge the chasm between them.

Diana went on to say that she and Charles had discussed with the family the possibility of separation, but it had caused such a panic that they had had to drop the whole idea. "So we're back to no-man's land . . ." I encouraged her to believe that when we are in a position in which we cannot change our fate, it does not mean that the situation will never change but that the moment has not yet come.

By great irony, I had narrowly missed meeting Charles some days before the Alps tragedy. At the beginning of March I was in Palm Beach, Florida, staying with Kathy Ford. Prince Charles was playing in a series of polo matches there and was the guest of honor at tea in the Trumps' home, Mar-A-Lago. Kathy was among twenty people who had been invited, and since I was her guest, I was also to go along. But at the last moment, Kathy was unwell and fate saw fit never to introduce the Prince to his wife's astrologer.

Just before I left for the States I had sent Diana some Bach flower remedies—sweet chestnut for despair, chicory for relaxation, and centaury for the "doormat syndrome." In my letter to her I suggested she might in extremis make a cocktail of all three. I had no conscious awareness at the time that she would shortly be facing yet another dark and painful passage.

On the face of it, my proximity to Charles days before the accident and my impulsive gift to Diana of some healing remedies appear to be unimportant. But they are what I would interpret as meaningful coincidences or synchronicities. It's as though a major event casts its shadow sometime beforehand and, if one is directly involved or linked to those who are involved, one unconsciously tunes in to that event and responds to it in some way. One might find the imprint of the event in a dream; there might be a marked sense of unease for no accountable reason, or one is drawn to be at a certain place at a specific time or take a certain action. People who are close to one another have an uncanny way of being alert to any impending danger. And while the individual involved in a crisis may send out alarm signals, rather like a surge of electricity, the precognition of an event suggests that the mind has an equal facility to reach forward in time as it does to dip into past events.

During that March phone conversation, Diana reiterated her conviction that it was Charles's fate not to become King—and hers not to become Queen. The tragedy at Klosters, when Charles was inches from death, gave that foreboding an alarming reality.

In May of the same year I sent Diana my finished chapter on Prince Charles for my forthcoming book,

Romancing the Stars. As usual, my heart was in my mouth in case she was offended at anything I had written. It was not just a courtesy to send Diana anything intended for publication but an absolute prerequisite. My overriding loyalty was to her as my client and someone I had come to be very fond of. Were she to take exception to anything, there would be no question of my including it.

Some of the more contentious aspects of the profile I was concerned about—or, rather, concerned about Diana's response towards—included:

Astrologically, 1988 looks to be a watershed for Charles. As transiting Saturn and Uranus oppose Uranus in his birth chart, the desire to be free to say and do as he wishes has never been stronger: So, too, are the burdens, responsibilities, and restrictions of his position . . . Breaking the rules (Uranus) comes with a heavy Saturnian cost. As future monarch, will he really be free to carry out the things he most wants to do: will he be allowed to challenge the status quo, which, as an uncompromising Scorpio, he will have to do if he is to help Britain become a better, more caring society? And even if he feels he can, will the powers that be permit such radical interference from a figurehead?

As an astrologer viewing the current planetary picture, one is tempted to speculate that Charles is finding increasing difficulty in blending his spiritual inner values with his outer role. In the process he is retreating further and further into himself, thereby widening the already large gulf between him and Diana . . .

The twist in the tail of my hypothesis is that a legal separation or divorce might become the very lever that would permit Charles to free himself in an entirely honorable fashion from the shackles and responsibilities of a role he does not in his heart of hearts want. After all, as King he would be the head of the Church of England—a position even in these enlightened times incompatible with being a divorced man . . . Give the simmering situation enough time, it will surely bubble to the surface—and as far as the astrology is concerned, we would be looking toward the early 1990s.

Charles has been preparing to become King all his life, but like the Prince of Wales before him, Edward VIII, he may believe he can have his cake and eat it. In Charles's case it is not the woman of his choice who is unacceptable, but the very things he stands for and the things he cares about. Paradoxically, free of kingly office, he may ultimately be the effective force he truly wants to be.

Several astrologers, both past and present, have also suggested that Charles might not become King. While in these uncertain times, accident or assassination cannot be ruled out of such forecasts, I consider the above scenario to be the most plausible.

To my surprise, Diana had found the chapter "riveting" and she saw no reason to change anything. However, the material had raised certain issues that she felt extremely strongly about. Whereas before, in the autumn of 1987, the prospect of a divorce from Charles was a welcome one, now she felt very differently. Her reservations centered on the effect a divorce would have on William and Harry. She was adamant that her own deeply unhappy experience of a family torn apart meant that she could not possibly do the same thing to her own children. Nevertheless, she realized that there was no way her marriage could be turned around. There had been too much damage on both sides. Yet again, the only answer seemed to lie in waiting for fate to intervene.

In the chapter I had sent her, I had earmarked the years 1991–1993 as a period of extreme crisis for the royal family, with the separation or divorce of Diana and Charles acting as the catalyst. What concerned Diana most was not how she would weather the crisis but how she could survive the intervening years. She could not bear the thought of waiting until 1993 to be "relieved of duty." Five years seemed a long day's journey into the dark night of the soul.

In November of 1988, my presentiments about the demise of the royal marriage and its destabilizing effect on the monarchy surfaced in the newspapers. The *Daily Mail* extracted from my chapter on Prince Charles and led with a banner headline BORN NOT TO BE KING. It was a sensational article, made even more sensational by the fact that such carefully worded phrases as "This is just a hypothesis" and "I'm like a weather forecaster putting two and two together in an attempt to make four" were left out, as was the fact that my statements were taken from a book published that month. The article gave the impression that in an effort to gain publicity, I had contacted the newspaper with a controversial prediction. More to the point, since the article discussed my association with the Faculty of Astrological Studies and maintained that my prediction was one shared by other notable astrologers, it caused a hurricane of outrage from the serious astrological faction.

Within days I had received a brusque letter from the president, Lindsay Radermacker, and a copy of letters sent by her on behalf of the Faculty to the *Daily Mail,* the *Times,* and Prince Charles. The aim of these letters was to distance the Faculty from me and my prediction about Charles and Diana and to point out that by speaking out about a notable public figure, I had breached the Faculty's code of ethics.

The issue provoked a furor in astrological circles. Letters were flying between the vice president and myself, and a special meeting was held to see what kind of damage limitation exercise should be launched since the good name of serious astrology was now in jeopardy. In the end, it took a threat from me to involve solicitors to quieten things down.

However, in royal circles, not an eyebrow was raised. A little while after the article had appeared, Diana rang me to sympathize with my predicament.

Even without the benefit of having seen the original text some months beforehand, she said she knew newspaper "hype" when she saw it. She reassured me that no one (i.e., the palace) had taken exception to the article and urged me to contact her in the event of any further dramas. It was also during this phone call on the twenty-ninth of November that she disclosed her real time of birth. Up until then, I, like all astrologers, had been using a time of 7:45 P.M. But according to her mother, Diana was born "just before the start of play at Wimbledon—a little after 2:00 P.M."

This, of course, was the time of birth originally given out by the Palace Press Office when Diana first arrived on the royal scene. So, either by accident or design, astrologers had been forced to work with totally the wrong chart. This "new" time now placed the lovely Libra on the Ascendant—which certainly made more sense given that Diana had become the world's most famous cover girl. And the presence of the harsh taskmaster of the zodiac, Saturn, in the fourth house of home and family added extra weight to Diana's childhood heartache and subsequent struggle with fears of rejection and abandonment.

But to return to the *Daily Mail* article. "Born Not to Be King" captured the public imagination, and I found myself the subject of a certain amount of hate mail. Even Barbara Cartland phoned me saying how appalled she was that I was promoting the demise of the monarchy. I also found myself on the opposite podium to several leading astrologers. In a debate with Jonathan Cainer on the radio 4 program "Loose Ends," Jonathan hotly argued that (a) the Prince and Princess of Wales were an ideal match and there was nothing wrong with their marriage, (b) they most certainly would not separate, and (c) Charles would be King. However, Jonathan explained, because the day Charles became sovereign would by implication be the day the Queen died, he was absolutely unprepared to disclose when Charles would ascend to the throne.

Before I began to spend increasing amounts of time studying the monarchy's charts, I had never seriously considered Charles not making it to the throne. But, as I explain in the previous chapter, the more one focuses on a chart, the sharper one's perception becomes. It may be that one is indeed tuning into the Greater Mind and therefore able to make quantum leaps in understanding denied to one in normal everyday consciousness. But certainly the more I dwelt upon Charles's chart, the less I felt he would become King.

At the time of his birth in 1948 some astrologers were already questioning the likelihood of Charles fulfilling his kingly destiny. Even the great Charles Carter had voiced such an opinion. The astrological culprit, according to Carter, was a poorly placed Jupiter. However, it was not so much Jupiter—or its reduced effect in Charles's chart—that was the problem as I saw it, but the placing of Neptune.

At the moment of Charles's birth, Neptune was right at the base of the horoscope—the Immum Coeli, or IC, to use its correct term. This area of the horoscope reveals the individual's heritage, his parentage—most particularly the father—and family life. And although Neptune is an intensely spiritual influence, its most usual effect in this area of the horoscope is to indicate some loss, sacrifice, or suffering linked to the family. Some individuals with this placement have a rather "unreal" childhood and their perception of the father figure in particular is clouded: it's the absent-father principle personified. Now, Charles's background is redolent with all these images—a father whom he idolized yet feared, a nonordinary upbringing that must have denied him a real sense of childhood. But more important, Charles is not just any individual. His roots, as delineated by the IC, represent the ancient line of the monarchy itself—and its future. So the theme of Neptunian loss and sacrifice is embodied by Charles: He has inherited such a theme and is therefore destined to play it out.

And he is not the first.

Edward VIII, who abdicated in 1936 and nearly brought about the collapse of the monarchy in the process, also had Neptune at the base of his chart. And, as if to underline the connection between the two Princes of Wales, they share the same Ascendant-Descendant axis—Edward had three degrees of Aquarius rising while Charles has five degrees of the same sign setting. Edward, of course, gave up the throne in order to marry the woman he loved, whereas it is Charles's very failure to love the woman he married that may ultimately cost him the throne.

But the comparisons between the charts of the two

Princes of Wales really begin and end with Neptune. Edward, as a sun Cancer with an albatross of a moon-Pluto square, was a mother-needing, mother-dominated individual. He was charismatic but weak. However, with a debonair fifth house sun in perfect harmony with his moon in Pisces, he would have been a popular King had he been allowed to fulfill his heritage. And while the opinion among many astrologers and historians alike has been that he never wanted to be King and his unacceptable love affair with twice-divorced Wallis Simpson provided the perfect way out of a job he never wanted, there is a distinct possibility, as I discuss in Chapter VIII, that he was maneuvered out of the way by the Establishment.

And maybe we have an echo of this today with the crisis of confidence in the monarchy largely brought about by Charles, his failed marriage, and his liaison with Camilla Parker Bowles. But more about the demise of the monarchy later.

Shortly before Christmas 1993, I was invited to join in a debate over Prince Charles on the Anglia television show "The Time, the Place." Despite the release of a tape earlier in the year containing an embarrassing exchange of endearments between Charles and Camilla Parker Bowles, Ingrid Seward, the editor of the British magazine *Majesty,* referred to the relationship between the Prince and Mrs. Parker Bowles as *alleged.* Strictly speaking, she was entirely correct to do so since neither Charles, Camilla, nor the palace had made any statement to the effect that the voices on the tape were who they were purported to be. However, in the public's mind there is no doubt as to the authenticity of the voices, and if Diana's comments directly to me are to be believed, Charles and Camilla not only had a relationship some years before his marriage to Diana, but the love affair was ongoing at the time of the wedding and beyond.

Most people have a "type" to whom they are attracted time and time again, and this can be perceived not only in the physical characteristics of the love object but in his or her astrological features. In my work I am constantly coming across individuals whose most important romantic and sexual relationships have been with people who belong to the same sun sign or the same astrological family of Cardinal, Fixed, or Mutable. Thus, it was no great surprise to me that Camilla's chart turned out to be almost a mirror image of Diana's.

Born some fourteen years earlier, practically to the day, Camilla, like Diana, is a sun Cancer. More to the point, Camilla's moon in Aquarius is a mere three degrees away from Diana's, so the two of them are classic hot-cold temperaments—the nearer you get, the more they crave independence; the further you retreat, the more they clamor for love and attention. They are both tenacious, persistent, manipulative, and strong-willed. They are both capable of infidelity, but only if their partner has failed them deeply. But Camilla always had the advantage. She was older and more *au fait* with the ways of men, and more particularly the ways of men like Charles. She learned through her abortive attempt to persuade Charles to propose to her that the best way to his heart was to be unobtainable. And to never create a show-stopping scene.

Diana's chart has a strongly Uranian content, which is what makes her emotionally volatile and unlikely to stay the course of a marriage, should it prove unfulfilling. She has a wayward streak. Camilla, with her Venus close to Uranus, will similarly not put up with a union she finds stifling; she is capable of flouting convention and seeking the extraordinary in life and love. Both women have the Cancerian need for a close, supportive, and loving relationship and a fulfilling family life, yet the Uranian influence also generates a tremendous thirst for independence— even if it means breaking some rules in the process.

Contrary to Camilla's conservative appearance and the admirable discretion with which she has conducted her relationship with Charles, she is nonetheless capable of just as many emotional games and unpredictable mood changes as Diana. But that is probably a side of her Charles has never seen.

Charles's relationship with Camilla has worked because he cannot truly belong to her, nor she to him. And this is first and foremost an astrological judgment. Uranus is an equally strong feature of Charles's chart, given that it presides over the whole area of close intimate encounters. Charles is a romantic with an utterly idealized view of women. Even more than a physical love, he craves a spiritual bond—a soul-to-soul union of the Tristan and Isolde kind. Yet he also relishes his bachelor existence. Therefore, women he can't have but whom he can yearn for and dream about fit the bill perfectly. While Camilla is not legally bound to him, nor he to her, their relationship can flower eternally. Camilla would have almost certainly presented her best face to Charles whenever they had some precious time together—and vice versa. And both of them, of course, had a common "enemy" in the form of Diana. However, the tables could easily have been reversed. Had Charles married Camilla when he was free to do so, then encountered Lady Diana Spencer, it might have all been very different. And it would have been Camilla who turned into the "dragon of a wife" while Diana remained the beautiful, unobtainable object of perpetual desire.

However, Camilla has one overriding astrological factor that was bound to give her the edge on Diana, and that is the placing of her Jupiter close to Charles's sun in Scorpio. This contact would bring out the best in both people—they are effectively a mutual admiration society. They each make the other feel good. And that is an abiding feature. With all sorts of upheaval in the relationship area of Camilla's chart in 1995 and 1996, it is highly possible that her marriage to Andrew Parker Bowles will come completely adrift. And with Jupiter bestowing all sorts of happiness and expansion in both Charles's and Camilla's charts in 1997, it would not be out of the question for them to cement their relationship in more formal terms—or maybe a reconciliation is nearer the mark.

On January 30, 1994, the British Sunday newspapers carried front-page stories over Charles's severance of all links with Mrs. Parker Bowles. According to friends and close associates of the Prince, he and Camilla had not seen each other for just over a year, although they had continued to talk regularly on the phone. This explosive and very public "dumping" of Mrs. Parker Bowles came in the wake of yet another near-death experience for Charles. On Wednesday, January 26, while the Prince was in Sydney, Australia, presenting prizes to schoolchildren at Tumbalong Park, a university student ran from the crowd firing shots from a gun in the direction of the Prince. The shots turned out to be blanks, and Charles's composure was admirable in the circumstances. Within hours of this alarming spectacle, some ten thousand miles away on a ski slope at Val d'Isere, a massive avalanche claimed the lives of five British skiers.

Echoes of the past—*foreshadows* of the future?

V

Foreshadows of the Future

Around 4:00 P.M. on June 28, 1990, Prince Charles took a heavy fall from his pony, Echo, while playing polo at Cirencester. He broke his arm badly and was taken to the local hospital, where, despite being in great pain, he insisted on waiting his turn in the emergency room.

"It's as if he's really jinxed, Penny," Diana was to say to me some five days later. "And if things go in threes, what's going to be the next? Will that be 'it'?"

As had been the custom over the preceding three years, on July 1 I would accompany her birthday card and gift with an astrological appraisal of the coming year. Either the same day or a little later, she would phone and we would discuss matters in greater depth. On this occasion, Charles was the main topic of conversation. Yet again, Diana had rallied to the call of the caring wife by presenting herself at his bedside as soon as she was permitted—rather different from as soon as she would have liked—and she was there, when he was discharged, to pick him up and drive him to Highgrove. But, yet again, any affection and care she might have given him was brushed aside. She drove back to London almost immediately in the certain knowledge that Mrs. Parker Bowles, who lived a few miles away, would be taking her place.

Three weeks later, Diana rang me again. Charles was not recovering from his injury as well or as quickly as he had hoped, and the prospect of his being unable to play polo again was deeply depressing for him. According to Diana, he was intolerable to live with, moody, unapproachable—impossible. During the phone call, in light of her musings over events happening in threes, she was to remind me of a conversation we had had a few days before Christmas or, more particularly, the two dreams I had discussed with her.

Dreams are more than the stuff of mindless imaginings. Clearly an element of sifting through day-to-day events and processing our experience is part and parcel of the function of dreams. But a dream is much more than a psychological shuffling process. In a dream's cryptic imagery lies not only the inner landscape of the psyche in the Jungian sense, but the shadows of past and future events.

In the summer and autumn of 1989, I had what

Jung might have termed two "big dreams." In the first, I was in the front row of an audience watching a play. The curtain went up and on the stage, sitting at a large desk, was Her Majesty, the Queen. She was delivering a somber speech, but no matter how hard I tried, I couldn't hear what she was saying. I knew only that it concerned the future of the monarchy. My eyes were then drawn to Charles and Diana, who were just behind her. They were posing for photographs and were seated—Charles behind Diana—on a child's rocking horse. Diana was laughing and Charles was urging her to be more responsible and to look serious for the cameras. There was a flash and a large explosion. All that was left on the stage was an empty car seat on a raised dais.

In the second dream, which I will recount in the present tense since that is how I recorded it in my diary, I am sitting in a sand dune having a picnic. Diana comes towards me, dressed in white with a black cloak around her. She sits down beside me. I feel awkward and unprepared for her sudden and unannounced arrival. She is telling me about someone called Peter who has been fired because of her. Apparently he is going to France and will be undergoing plastic surgery to conceal his identity. She goes on to talk to me about William, and while she does this, she holds up a large figure 3. She then begins to cry, and I comfort her, urging her not to give up on the marriage. She recovers her composure and I take up the topic of Peter, referring to him as a *past* relationship. "It's not over. It's very much on," she says.

The scene changes to my then home, Bramshott Court. Diana comes into the sitting room with a large gift-wrapped present, which she hands to me. When I open it, I find a strange-looking object about three feet in size—the only thing this object vaguely resembles is the ornate hand of a large clock. I am embarrassed at the enormity of the gift and refuse it, saying Prince Charles might be cross if she gave it away. I escort her out to her car, and when I return, William is seated in the same chair. He is much older and sporting a beard. He says to me, "They don't tell me everything, you know. For a few minutes we lost complete radio contact with them . . ." As he was saying this to me, I saw an event from an aerial point of view. Two police motorcycles and a white car streaming ahead, leaving a black car on its own. Two vans approach from either side and prevent the black car from moving forward. The dream ends in chaos and I hear my own voice saying, "Isn't anyone going to do anything . . . ?"

Analysts will clearly have a field day with the offerings of my own personal unconscious here, but aside from taking the dreams apart on a strictly psychological level, there are some intriguing fore-tastes of the future here—and the past.

During our December '89 conversation, the topic of reincarnation had come up. Diana confided that she was becoming more and more deeply involved in a spiritual path that she not only believed was her role in this life but something she had done in a past existence. Given that "Peter" was a key figure in the second dream and that we were by the sea, I wondered if there was an echo of the time of Christ here. "Oh, yes . . ." she said emphatically, "I was a martyr."

I will return to the premonitory aspects of these dreams in Chapter VIII, but suffice to say, the images in the second dream convey a wealth of information about the current state of play in Diana's life—more specifically that there was a strong possibility of an ongoing relationship. And while I am disinclined to disclose anything about Diana's liaisons at that time, other authors—Christopher Hutchins among them—have earmarked the summer of 1989 as the point at which her friendship with James Gilby really took off.

On May 3, 1989, in the wake of some near riots in Merseyside over the absence of any senior royal presence at the Hillsborough memorial service, I wrote to Diana to reassure her she was not in imminent danger of being hung, drawn, and quartered by a band of incipient revolutionaries.

I am frankly boggled at the amount of complex planetary activity in your chart at the moment. What I have done is look fairly closely at the next two months only, just to see where the major ups and downs are, so to speak . . . Uranus is particularly strong. This planet brings change and the unexpected: Since it is presently hooked up to your Mercury (movement, communication, speech, and travel), you can anticipate a degree of accident proneness and the sort of potentially dangerous situations that have erupted recently, as well as some truly enlightening experiences.

*The most important thing about this Uranus
activity is that now you can change your attitude
to long-term situations, thereby allowing for new
solutions and opportunities that will erase past
patterns and limitations. Indeed, the more you
recognize your need to express yourself in different ways and your ability to "do your own thing,"
the fewer disturbing things will happen to you.
"Accidents" are invariably signs that the psyche
needs to break out in a new direction and that
unconsciously you are blocking such a
process . . .*

*Near May 15 and June 12, there are strong
Venus contacts in your chart—at one end of the
spectrum we are looking at involvements with the
arts, beauty, fashion, etc., and at the other, love
and romance . . . You have a strong element of
fate working in your life, especially linked to your
relationships. While you will find it easier to give
in to your fate, accept the way things are, you are
not exactly powerless to do anything. I think the
intrinsic lesson to be learned from your relationships is that of power and control: On the one
hand, you have to experience how it feels to be in
someone else's power and control, and on the
other, you may find yourself in a relationship
where the boot is on the other foot. Yes, you must
find your own power, but it's not the power one
associates with throwing one's weight around or
insisting that others dance to your tune, but an
inner sense of power: By gaining complete com-*

mand of a situation (and I must stress that this is an inner thing, perhaps most clearly understood as a combination of attitude and centeredness), you are no longer at the mercy of a situation but able to transcend it. Just how much your destiny is linked to your relationships has already been shown by your marriage to Charles . . . but I'll say no more. By the way, continue to be careful whom you trust at the moment and avoid taking risks that could affect your reputation—Neptune, need I say more!

Although not stated directly in this letter, with Venus—the planet of, among other themes, love and romance—transiting her sun sign, the potential for love to blossom—or at the very least, a mild flirtation—was strong. However, coupled with such strong Uranian and therefore rather reckless aspects, the chances of love being suddenly rekindled with Charles were virtually nil, and the chances of someone new on the scene were high.

I knew Diana to be a romantic in every sense of the word. For a girl brought up on the Cartlandesque philosophy that all women want to be wooed and won without ever taking their clothes off, sex always promised to be a thorny rather than a rosy experience for Diana. And here she was married to an archetypal Scorpio to whom sex was inevitably the stuff of life; a man who wouldn't want to beat about the rosebush. I'm not saying that Diana ever volunteered the information that she was sexually unfulfilled, but during the course of our dialogues and my reading of the situation, it was clear that something was very definitely missing from this aspect of her life.

Diana's complex arrangement involving the moon, Uranus, and Venus in her natal chart is indicative of someone who is either very adventurous, inventive, and uninhibited where sex is concerned, or someone who is frightened to death of the whole business. Certainly it is the chart of a slow starter; someone who only after trial, error, and encouragement would be able to release her sexuality. It is my belief that this never happened with Charles, and was a large part of the reason for the added strain on their marriage. For many anorgasmic women, there is a desperate search for the key to unlock the doorway to sexual fulfillment. Yet all the restraints, emotional, psychological, and her position as the Princess of Wales, made this a treacherous and protracted process.

Diana has all the astrological hallmarks of a woman who is cut off from her sexual self and therefore puts on a great performance without feeling a thing. She is a marvelous anima figure for men. She embodies archetypally feminine attributes and is therefore capable of reflecting those things most men desire without being robbed of her essential self in the process. Certain men are captivated by a woman whom they can worship, a woman who has not given of herself entirely. She may be generous with gifts and with compliments, fun to be with, affectionate and adoring, but she does not release any sleeping serpent of real sexual passion because she is terrified of it herself.

And this is a two-way street. Because the men who enter into this "dance" are also likely to be threatened by a woman whose sexuality is lush and coming from a deep place, a relationship that fits neatly between the covers of a romantic novel suits them as well. The emotional risks of a fully realized relationship are too great for both people—at least until either or both has made a quantum emotional, psychological, or spiritual leap. Certainly the dialogue between Diana and James Gilby in the infamous "New Year's" telephone call gives every indication that Diana was playing at love, and James was perfectly cast as the devoted romantic hero (a role Charles could only muster for a brief period while under the spell of the anima). Diana's requirement in a man was that he show her love and support rather than fulfill any sexual vacuum. And, given the arid desert of her marriage, she can be forgiven for seeking such things elsewhere rather than becoming a martyr to them.

However, this foray into the ins and outs of Diana's love life has led us away from the main theme of this chapter, which concerns the forebodings over the future of the monarchy. In that same conversation of December 18, 1989, Diana voiced her fears that Charles would meet with some accident that would deny them both the throne. After recounting my dreams, which gave anything but the prospect of a sunny future for the monarchy, we went on to discuss the marriage. Back in August of that year Diana had told me that the one area in which the relationship had improved was that she and Charles could "now talk reasonably" over the phone and that he was "moving closer—about an inch a year!" However, the children were both aware something was badly wrong between them, and William had said, "We know Daddy makes you unhappy."

Nevertheless, a separation or a divorce had been absolutely ruled out. Diana said that she had always understood my ambivalence over the issue of the marriage since my astrological view led me to believe the marriage would not last, yet my personal belief was that everything possible should be done to make it work. During our conversation at the end of December Diana confessed that she had never watched an individual in such pain as Charles, who seemed almost suicidal in his distress at times. She even implied that he might well be happier to continue his work beyond the physical realm. That way, she opined, he could have more of an influence on his people than he might have as King.

By the time of his polo accident some six months later, Charles's emotional and spiritual pain was made even more unbearable by the physical discomfort he was experiencing. For weeks, whenever Diana and he were together, he was remote and sunk deep into himself. Diana made the comment to me in July that he appeared to be in self-destruct mode, and given the increasing sense of fruitlessness of his role, she worried that something much worse would befall him. However, nothing did and gradually, by the autumn of 1990, life had returned to normal. Hostilities stabilized at just above freezing point.

Shortly after Charles's accident I was asked by Diana Hutchinson of the *Daily Mail* for my views on Charles's future since, as an advocate of astrology herself, she wondered whether these two accidents in the space of two years were indicative of some kind of jinx. She also wondered whether rumors of Charles sinking into a serious depression could be borne out in the astrology. And I agreed to provide her with a short article. In the event, the article never appeared, sad because it came the nearest to painting an accurate portrait of what is now past history.

Prince Charles's chart shows him to be a man of great authority and depth. He'd be a marvelous King for the demands of the twenty-first century. He's highly spiritually motivated and very committed to humanitarian issues.

Now, and for some time, however, he has been in a deep depression—what we might call the dark night of the soul. He may not interpret how he is feeling in this way, but it is clear that he is a man unfulfilled and groping for some kind of solution to his existential dilemma. He may well require some help with this depression, for if it is correctly processed, he could emerge from this tunnel a greater man. He would make a positive gain from his suffering and he would become more substantial because of it.

In this same way—making a virtue out of a difficulty—the powerful astrological influences affecting him and the monarchy through 1991, 1992, and 1993 would act as a sort of "birthing" process to a new regime. Astrologically speaking, it is Pluto, the planet of transformation, that brings this theme into being since this planet is going to conjoin Charles's sun, the Queen's Midheaven, and contact Princess Diana's moon, Venus, and Uranus—not to mention major features of the rest of the royal family's charts. This transit of Pluto underlines the whole argument between destiny and free will. If there is such a thing as free will, then now is the time for Charles and the monarchy to exercise it. In other words, the royal family needs to recognize that fundamental changes in their structure must occur. This is not just a matter of PR but of acquiescing to the changing times. I don't pretend to have any answers as to how this must come about— although the obvious issue of the Queen's paying tax is a major opportunity—but I am convinced that if they do not make some dramatic changes in the style of the monarchy, fate will force their hand. In other words, we may see extraordinary events unfolding that affect the Constitution in a profound and irrevocable way.

In 1936 there was another constitutional crisis. On January 20, 1936, George V died, and in keeping astrologically with such a momentous event, the sun was at the opposite end of the zodiac to Pluto, which in turn made pivotal contacts to Edward's chart—most notably in the area of family, father, and heritage. Some ten days beforehand an eclipse in mid-Capricorn-Cancer had made portentous links to all three charts of Great Britain and Edward's Saturn. There were four eclipses during 1936—the final one on December 11, a matter of days before the abdication of Edward VIII, clearly acting as a signature of that epoch-making event.

In 1992 and 1993 we have a similar pattern of eclipses affecting leading members of the royal family's charts and those of Great Britain. And we can look to the key months of December 1991, January 1992, June 1992, December 1992, and November 1993. Of all these, the eclipses of the winter of 1991/92 and November 1993 are the most vital. And perhaps we can see this as a distinct cycle of events that have their beginning in December of 1991 and culminate in December of 1993.

I consider the planetary portents of these two years to be greater than those of 1936. While the monarchy may well withstand the hurricane that hits it, its fabric will be fundamentally changed. Pluto is symbolized by the phoenix rising out of the ashes. In this way we can look positively toward the coming two years in that something new will be born out of the ashes of the old. Some things will have to pass away at this time for the new to take root.

Almost a year to the day after Charles's polo accident, William was rushed unconscious to the hospital after being struck on the head with a golf club. The injury was serious enough to warrant immediate surgery, but fortunately there was no lasting damage. Indeed, the more serious damage incurred was to Charles's image. Entirely in character, and, of course, like any other devoted mother in the same situation, Diana spent every waking hour by William's bedside. Charles, however, once he had established that William was in no danger, elected to fulfill a previous engagement that same night at the opera at Covent Garden.

A few days after William's accident, Diana phoned, quite naturally feeling insecure about the future after William's quite awful experience. And I promised to send her a rundown of the year ahead. I sent her some books for her birthday and, in the accompanying letter, reassured her by reiterating what I had said. "The accident occurred at quite an astrologically stressed time, although William's chart looked strong and positive. And I'm sure this brush with fate will leave no lasting scars, physically, emotionally, or psychologically."

Diana, you are now on the threshold of all those mightily important times that we discussed all those years ago. Uranus has already cleared away much of the old pain and uncertainty in your life and to some degree created a sort of "new" Diana. All the difficulties (and the joys) you have been through during the last few years have been preparing you for this next stage. You could not possibly have met the events that look set to occur during the next three years without this sort of "baptism of fire."

As you know, I'm not a fatalist or a seer. I look at the charts and attempt to unravel what a particular set of planets may mean in a person's life at any time—past or future. As I cast my eyes over the charts of the principal members of the royal family, I can see that you all have planets toward the end of the Fixed signs (Taurus, Leo, Scorpio, and Aquarius). Pluto, with his transformative signature, is poised to contact these planets over the next three years, and by the end of that time, what was once the status quo and thought to be completely unchanging and unchangeable will have been radically altered. If you keep the theme of death and rebirth—the phoenix rising out of the ashes of a situation—you may be able to glimpse in the symbolism what you and the family will have to go through. Using an allegory leaves the events free to present themselves in whatever form, just as long as they evoke the process of transformation.

Sometime during this three-year period, there are likely to be some changes in the structure of the family, and together with political instability, not to mention Britain's entry into the Common Market, England will be very different by the mid-nineties. Somehow, the family has a crisis to *face about its role, and all sorts of events, both within the family and outside it (politically), will contribute to this crisis. Things cannot stay the same. But, positively, a "death" of the old always precedes the birth of the new.*

As you know, I have always been concerned about Charles's chart during these times. As Pluto draws ever nearer his sun (exactitude occurs next year in the spring and late November/early December), he seems already to be a man groping his way through a long tunnel, not knowing if there will be a light at the end of it. Around this Christmas (1991) and the New Year, there are indications that something very powerful is going on—perhaps behind the scenes—and to some degree it is what happens around this time that sets the stage for how transformed he and his life are to be. There is an eclipse on a highly sensitive point of his chart on December 21 (1991) and another on January 4, 1992. If this were happening in my chart, or any of my family's, I would be particularly vigilant around the few weeks straddling these dates. Successfully past this volcanic zone, I wouldn't rest on my laurels. I would be aware that a new order was desperately trying to assert itself, and if I couldn't or wouldn't get behind those things that needed to be changed, fate would sort it out for me instead and I would have no control over matters.

At the same time, you, too, are experiencing some Plutonic transformation, and I imagine, despite the brilliant job you're doing of making everything look like a breeze, you are deeply aware that "something's got to give"—and sooner rather than later. I don't know how much longer you can "sit" on some of these simmering situations, and it may be, contrary to your belief that your marital ship can (in the form you have now accepted) carry you across the next thirty years, its leaky base may not prove up to the job! This coming period (with its center-point of December 1992) is make or break time for roles and relationships.

There's a joke I heard recently, by the way, that might be appropriate here:

Do you want to make God laugh?

Tell Him your plans!

The moon, Venus, Uranus, and Neptune are all being activated in your chart from now on, and this may have different effects on all levels of your life from the home base—your own four square walls—to your family (Spencer) and your feelings and emotions. There are some glorious, happy moments attached to these themes, yet also some sadness. If a new order enters your own life, it inevitably means that something must pass away. Nevertheless, Jupiter is determined that you should have some great happiness and love in your life, and "he" is very active in the late summer and early autumn.

I have a feeling that you may consult others who can tune in to future events. If I can give you these times (December 1991 and January–March and December 1992), he or she may be able to give you a sharper angle on things.

On reading the material I had sent her, Diana said she could not imagine what events would take place to change the status quo—certainly not in the marriage —but she could identify all too easily with the feeling that "something's got to give." She also told me quite emphatically that she consulted no one else. I was her only astrologer and the only person she would trust in this way.

Shortly after Christmas, the first rumblings of the Plutonic volcano were beginning to make themselves felt. On January 2, 1992, some twelve days after an eclipse on Charles's Jupiter-Uranus opposition, I received an early morning call from Diana.

"Well, we got through the eclipse all right," she said.

"There may be no actual event to mark this eclipse," I said, "but it very definitely means *something.*"

"Oh, well, there was Her Majesty's speech . . . It was a shock to us all, especially my husband."

The part in the Queen's Christmas message to the country to which Diana was referring was the heavily underlined statement that the Queen saw her reign as a job for life: no prospect of abdication. Until that moment, according to Diana, Charles had believed she would one day abdicate in his favor. With the prospect of many more years in the wilderness,

Charles entered a deep depression, cutting himself off from the rest of the family for five days.

Diana and I went on to discuss the points I had made some six months before about the monarchy having to get behind its own transformation. "The family are living in the past, Penny—they're totally unaware they need to change . . ." Diana's greatest fear, however, was that she would be the agent of that change. She was truly worried that it would be her who "tipped everything on its head." I reassured her that whatever was going to happen would take place with or without her input. However, in my notes on that phone call I have added: "Privately I consider she will, wittingly or unwittingly, be the catalyst." On a lighter note, Diana told me that Fergie had become quite good at the tarot cards, the eerie factor being the Tower—a card indicating upheaval, even catastrophe —kept coming up time and time again in both their spreads. "My marriage isn't the only one in disarray . . ." she was to add. It was also during that telephone call that I told Diana that I was joining *Today* newspaper as their astrologer and hoped that my position in "Fleet Street" wouldn't damage our friendship. "Great!" she responded. "We'll be able to meet up more."

Of course, quite the reverse was to happen. And, although I did not realize it at the time, I had suddenly become a very valuable pawn in a chess game of Machiavellian proportions.

VI

Distance:
Lens Disenchantment

For the royal family, 1992 began as it meant to go
on—in a blaze of scandal, if not a bonfire of insani-
ties.

On January 15 the *Daily Mail* carried a front-page
story cantering on a sensational series of pictures
discovered at a smart Cadogan Square address. One
hundred twenty photographs in all pictured the Duchess of York with Texan Steve Wyatt and her children,
Beatrice and Eugenie, clearly enjoying a holiday in the
sunshine. In fact, the photographs were taken in May
of 1990 at a luxury villa on the Mediterranean.
However shocking the revelations that Sarah had
spent a holiday with a dashing American while her
husband was on Navy exercises, what the incident
clearly revealed, and in the most public way pos-

sible, was that all was far from well in the Yorks' marriage.

In truth, there had been a great deal wrong with the Yorks' marriage for some considerable time. And however scandalous the release of the holiday photographs in 1992 proved, they were not half as potentially damaging as some taken in the early part of 1987—a mere six months after Andrew and Sarah had been married in Westminster Abbey.

In the spring of 1987 a man I shall refer to as Paul was contacted by a Walter Mittyesque person called Sebastian Shore. Paul, a colorful figure capable of blending into the criminal underworld as easily as the huntin', shootin', and fishin' circles, works closely with M16. Sebastian excitedly informed Paul that he had some "dynamite" photographs of the Duchess of York taken at a party at Bubbles Rothermere's flat in central London. The photographs were purported to show Sarah in an intimate embrace with an alleged yuppie drug dealer.

Paul's first step was to contact Detective Constable Tom Reed at Scotland Yard and inform him of the conversation and the existence of some deeply embarrassing photographs of the Duchess of York. Paul next contacted the late Trevor Kempson, chief crime reporter of the *News of the World,* who also worked hand in hand with British Intelligence. Paul and Trevor had known each other since 1980 when the two mounted a campaign to bring to the attention of the public the security risk mobile phones presented. I shall go

further into this issue in the next chapter. But suffice it
to say that whenever matters of a sensitive nature
concerning the royal family or any notable public
figure fell into Paul's hands, his first call was to the
police. From there, Paul would invariably act as
go-between, gathering information from those trying
to "sell" and those who were prepared to "buy," but
with constant police monitoring of the situation.

Within an hour of Paul's call to Detective Constable
Tom Reed, Chief Superintendent Alec Ross contacted
Paul to arrange a meeting. They met later that day on
the M 25 at Potters Bar. By this time, it had been
established that the photographs were genuine and
that they had to be recovered at all costs.

From then on, in order to retain his "street cred"
among the criminal underworld, Paul was on his own.
Knowing full well that no paper would dare print such
outrageous photographs, he nevertheless had to make
the first moves in order to get a kind of Dutch auction
going. That way, the police could legitimately begin
their operation not only to recover the photographs
but to rout out a drug dealer or two. A week or so later,
Trevor, representing the *News of the World,* met with
Sebastian and Paul, and although the photographs did
not change hands, they were seen and a figure of thirty
thousand pounds per photograph was discussed.

To cut a long story short, it took until the summer
for the situation to reach its conclusion. By that time,
events were rapidly turning into a farce. A colleague of
the man in the photos with Sarah—allegedly *his*
supplier of cocaine—leapt out of a window to escape

a posse he believed to be the police at his front door. A little later, as he was being taken by ambulance to the local hospital, a group of men pursued the vehicle along Norwood High Street, shooting at it in broad daylight. Needless to say, all this high-profile activity did nothing to smooth the passage of the photographs into safe hands. And, shortly before the pictures were due to be handed over, they were mysteriously stolen. To this day, they have never surfaced. But you can be sure they are somewhere with a little time bomb ticking away gently underneath them.

So, in many ways, some rather pretty snaps by a pool in front of a charming villa was a positive PR exercise in comparison to the "Rothermere collection." And even those that surfaced later in the year by yet another pool, this time with Texan Johnny Bryan, pale in contrast with those taken in 1987. And, although no one wants to throw brickbats at Sarah, she took the most absurd risks for someone in her position. And maybe there is some cause to believe that right from the outset, in a similar vein to her father, Major Ron, who, among many other acts of sheer lunacy, signed his own name at one of London's most notorious massage parlors, she had her finger poised permanently above the self-destruct button.

Certainly her chart would bear this out, although I have to admit that when I first met her, I was enchanted by her and, from our dialogues, considered her Scorpio self-destruct side would be counteracted by her more Arian survivalist qualities. As it is, the headstrong Aries side of her has combined with the

Scorpio to propel her along a course of disaster to disaster and from one dangerous liaison to another.

Sarah may be a sun Libran—a sign with all the charm and haute couture of Betsy Bloomingdale—but her moon in Aries and the close proximity of feisty Mars to the sun give her the restraint of Attila the Hun. Mars-Aries women love to do things like learning to fly helicopters. They love to win. They thrive on challenge and daring. Put them in a pair of white gloves and a silk frock and within ten minutes they'll have caught the hem on a coffee table and accidentally stuck their fingers in the honey. Indeed, on our first meeting in a Notting Hill Gate restaurant, Sarah was sporting a king-size safety pin in the hem of her skirt. As I mentioned earlier, I had strong reservations about the durability of Sarah and Andrew's marriage since Sarah's chart did not reflect Andrew's ideal counterfoil—and vice versa. However, Sarah's chart had many zodiac degrees in common with the royal family. And it was this factor, rather more than anything else, that enabled me to encourage her to believe that she would become one of their number—obviously by marriage to Andrew. And in the run up to their engagement I spent many telephone sessions reassuring her that she and Andrew would make it to the altar—and, more important, telling her how to get him there, at one point giving her almost a day-by-day account of what to do and what not to do. Patience and trust are not Sarah's strongest suits.

Straddling the Midheaven of her chart are Venus and Pluto—a combination that, on the one hand, describes a woman whose destiny will be profoundly linked to her love life and, on the other, a female who, with her passionate nature, has the capacity to affect other people in a deep and profound way. In the light of history, we can also see that her love affairs, conducted in the full glare of the camera lens, have not only dramatically affected her image (also represented by the Midheaven) but contributed to her fall from royal grace.

Despite the strong Scorpio-Pluto themes in Sarah's chart, she clearly operates from her impulsive Mars spirit. What also appears to interfere with her ability to judge a situation correctly and see at least a couple of moves along the chessboard is the placing of Mercury (the planet of thought and communication) next to delusion-packed Neptune—and in the confusing and mysterious twelfth house of the horoscope. Given a different setting, and maybe a few more years, all these same astrological factors could lead Sarah to make some very powerful discoveries about herself, which will in turn produce a very compassionate, spiritual, and self-sacrificing woman. Indeed, her love and support when anyone she loves hits a major and very public crisis have been evident on more than one occasion. She's the type to go down with the ship, if she believes in it and it has claimed her heart.

Perhaps her actions and her public humiliation are already the Neptunian sacrifice she has paid for her need to live a fulfilled life. And, maybe, she has been a victim of the royal system. But what she has most certainly done is play into the hands of those who would not wish her well. But this all seems a far cry from the spring and summer of 1986 when she was ensconced in Buckingham Palace and preparing for the Big Day on July 23. I had lunch with Sarah in her apartment in the Palace on May 6. It was a mixture of business and pleasure. Sarah had very kindly agreed to be included as one of the profiles in my book *Romancing the Stars,* and we needed to discuss aspects of her life in regard to her birth chart. She was even sporting enough to allow me to record the interview on cassette tape so that I wouldn't make any errors when it came to writing the piece itself. Two very different images are etched in my memory of this meeting: a lewd, but nonetheless hilarious, book on the sexual antics of frogs which leapt out at me from the top of a pile on her sitting room table—a sort of amphibian *Kama Sutra*—and one of the most delicious crème brûlées I can ever remember eating.

As we munched our way through the meal, Sarah went back over her early life. However, the main part of the discussion centered on her feelings for Andrew and her need to be loved. She was very clearly over her affair with Paddy McNally, which had run a very volatile course over the three years between 1982 and 1985, and very definitely in love with Andrew.

When I came to write the profile itself, I did my best to be fair to the Sarah I had come to like, and at the same time true to the astrology.

There are three entirely different themes in Sarah's chart, which sometimes have great difficulty in working together. Sarah's Libra side can be lazy, hedonistic, and too accommodating at times: She may rely too heavily on others, seeking their opinions and reactions before making her own. Her Aries-Mars side is precisely the opposite, indicating she is too impulsive and hasty on occasion, with a tendency to rush in where angels fear to tread. The Scorpio-Pluto influence adds a certain obsessiveness to her nature, even some secrecy: She can be stubborn, with a tendency to make mountains out of molehills. Sarah has the potential to be a wonderful and loyal friend but a dangerous enemy.

In keeping with her Mars spirit, she is marvelous in a crisis but abhors nonessentials. "Crisis is easy. It's the trivial I can't deal with." *Aries and Mars are to challenge and adventure what bees are to honey; and if the future looks uncomfortably bland, Sarah will seek out a crisis or two.*

Astrologically, Sarah emerges as the type who needs security and permanence in her relationships. She is a great romantic and requires constant reassurances that she is loved, adored— above and beyond anyone else. Sarah, with her Aries moon and Scorpio Ascendant, is not the sort to tolerate competition. Despite her confident outspoken personality, Sarah is insecure and emotionally vulnerable. Once in a relationship, she becomes dependent on the partner. Yet she realizes that by becoming so dependent on anyone, she increases her vulnerability—a sort of Catch 22 situation. Also, in typical Libran fashion, she can't decide which is more important—

*her independence or a sharing-caring relation-
ship.*

*On their engagement, Andrew and Sarah
stressed their ability to work as a team was a
major factor in their relationship . . . But like
any relationship, it's not perfect. In their relationship chart, like the Prince and Princess of Wales,
Uranus figures strongly. On the one level this
suggests their interaction is a volatile one and the
relationship will have huge peaks and troughs:
They may well encounter periods when they feel
"trapped" by their marriage, then others when
they feel totally at one with each other. On
another level, as a couple they may experience a
sudden change in the tide of their affairs—and
their roles could change dramatically . . .
Certainly Sarah's fear that a sense of complacen-
cy will develop in her marriage is singularly
unlikely . . .*

*With her Venus-Pluto conjunction on the high-
est point of her chart, there are indications that
her role will be anything but a minor one. When
Pluto, her chart ruler, crosses her Ascendant in the
early 1990s, some of this potential will be released. During this time almost all members of
the royal family show change and transformation
in their charts. What this ultimately means is not
for me to ponder upon and for us all to find out as
history unfolds . . .*

And by 1992, we all did indeed find out . . .

* * *

*D*iana courageously tries to win Charles's love in the face of uncertainty and insecurity. *(Photo by Tim Graham)*

*I*n one of her earliest meetings with me, I was moved when Diana said, "It's all right. I've always known I'd never be queen." *(Photo by Alpha)*

$\mathcal{E}$dward, of course, gave up the throne to marry the woman he loved, American Wallace Simpson, whereas it is Charles's very failure to love the woman he married that may ultimately cost him the throne. *(Top photo by Popperfoto, bottom photo by Rex Features)*

*S*arah Ferguson, the Duchess of York, and Prince Andrew on their wedding day. *(Photo by Tim Graham)*

*S*arah's note asked me to delete references that might upset her mother, which, of course, I did. *(Author's Collection)*

KENSINGTON
PALACE
19.12.90.

Dear Penny,

What a lovely surprise it was to get your book - Thank you so much for thinking of me at Christmas! ... What a year its been for this particular lady. Surprises around every corner!!

The title of the book is fascinating in itself so I much look forward to reading it.

A huge 'thank you', Penny, for my lovely present + much love to you + the team. Diana.

A letter of thanks from Diana. I received this note after I sent her a copy of my book *The Forces of Destiny*, published in May 1990. *(Author's Collection)*

Another note of thanks from Diana. This one came after I sent her a copy of my book *Divine Encounters*, which was published in November 1991. *(Author's Collection)*

𝒟 (crown logo)

KENSINGTON
PALACE

November 16th
1991.

Dear Penny,
    A very special thank you
for sending me 'Divine Encounters'.
I was thrilled to bits to

have been thought of &
so look forward to reading
your book – what a fascinating
subject & what an insight
for us readers!
I do hope that life is treating
you kindly & again a million
thanks, Penny, for such a
kind thought. With my love. Diana

TO you both.

Wishing you a very Happy Christmas
and New Year

with love from one few of us,

Diana

TO you All.

Wishing you a very Happy Christm
and New Year

with our love from

Diana.

TO Penny & her team!

Wishing you a very Happy Christmas
and New Year

with love from.

Diana.

To Penny & her team.

Wishing you a very Happy Christmas
and New Year

Love from us all,
Diana.

To you All,

Wishing you a very Happy Christmas
and New Year

from,
Diana and Charles

The Christmas cards I received annually from
Diana—Charles personally added his signature in
1987. *(Author's Collection)*

$\mathcal{M}$y perception of Diana was that she was not a princess who needed to be humored but rather a young woman desperate to replace despair with hope. The more I dwelled upon Charles's chart, the less I felt he would become king. *(Photo by Rex Features)*

$\mathcal{D}$iana attempts to fill the roles of adored public figure, wife, and mother. *(Photo by Rex Features)*

*U*nable to bear the increasing pressures upon her, Diana officially withdrew from public life with a prepared statement on December 3, 1993. *(Photo by Alpha)*

*D*iana's public mask cracks under strain. *(Photo by Alpha)*

*L*iz Nocon, Claire Park and others join me after the wedding of Sarah and Andrew. *(Author's Collection)*

$\mathcal{S}$arah with John Bryan, whom she described as her business advisor. Events would later prove he enjoyed a closer relationship with the Duchess of York. *(Photo by Alpha)*

Texan Steve Wyatt, another close friend of Sarah. (Photo by Alpha)

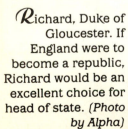

Richard, Duke of Gloucester. If England were to become a republic, Richard would be an excellent choice for head of state. (Photo by Alpha)

$\mathcal{S}$howing great promise as a young ballerina, the author later went on to join The Royal Ballet Company. *(Above photo from the Author's Collection, right photo by Michael Stannard)*

𝒯he author today. *(Photo copyright 1992 NEWS (UK) LTD.)*

Before committing the profile to my publishers, I sent Sarah a copy for her approval. In her written reply she asked that I delete certain statements that might be upsetting to her mother. However, we also had a long discussion over an original part of the text that voiced my concern over a configuration that could lead to gynecological problems. In my heart of hearts I wondered if she might have problems with pregnancies and childbirth. She went on to explain that her mother had suffered a miscarriage, and therefore she was terrified fate held the same in store for her. In the event, of course, Sarah went on to produce two beautiful daughters. However, it was alleged that she had had an early miscarriage in 1987 and was subsequently treated with a fertility drug. Furthermore, Beatrice's birth on 8–8–88 (at 8:18 P.M.!) was a traumatic one and, if rumors are to be believed, little Bea nearly didn't make it.

On July 23 Sarah and Andrew were married in Westminster Abbey. It was a glittering occasion and, although it was inconceivable at the time, probably the last royal wedding of such enormous pomp and ceremony that we will ever see. And I feel very privileged to have been there at the time and to have such happy memories of the day.

My husband, Simon, and I drove to the Abbey on that warm but cloudy morning. We had been sent a special sticker identifying us as guests, which we had been instructed to place on the windshield. All the roads surrounding Buckingham Palace and Whitehall had been cordoned off: Only the gilded coaches,

Horse Guards, wedding guests, and all the officialdom that accompanied the wedding were allowed access to the Abbey. As we came down Park Lane and entered Green Park, we heard a sound like the soft roar of the sea, way in the distance. Only when we rounded the corner into St. James's Park—the front of Buckingham Palace on our right—did we realize that sound of the sea was the roar of the crowds lining the pavements. As we continued down the Mall, people everywhere were waving. I turned round to see who was behind us because there was no other car in front and suddenly understood that the crowds were waving at us. It was simply the excitement and anticipation of the occasion. So I said to Simon, "Do you think we ought to wave back?" "Why not!" he replied. As soon as we did, the crowd went mad. And we just waved and waved our way to the Abbey! It was one of the most thrilling experiences of my life.

From our seats in the Abbey, it was impossible to see the altar. In fact, we were facing another bank of guests on the other side of the nave—I was almost directly opposite the film director Bryan Forbes and his wife, Nanette Newman. We had to wait some considerable time before Sarah arrived, but when she did, there was an audible gasp from us all. She looked absolutely beautiful. And the ceremony that followed sent quivers down the spine. There is nothing quite so spine-chilling as the sound of a matchless choir and orchestra echoing through the walls of one of the most beautiful and ancient abbeys in the world. The whole experience was out of this world.

On our way out of the Abbey, we met the proverbial wall of photographers. Hundreds and hundreds of lenses pointing at anyone leaving the ceremony; and a constant click-clicking of camera shutters. I could get used to this, I thought . . .

Only family and those closest to the royal family were invited to the wedding breakfast at the Palace after the ceremony. My husband and I joined the Nocons, Albert Watson (who had been chosen by Andrew to take the official photographs of the wedding), Clare Park and Katie Rabbet (two of Andrew's ex-girlfriends) for our own bash at Joe Allen's in Covent Garden.

Shortly after the Yorks' return from their honeymoon, I rang Sarah at Buckingham Palace. I had inadvertently considered myself a friend and made the huge mistake of picking up the phone to her as in times past. Almost as soon as I had uttered the word "hello," I knew something had very definitely changed. Her voice was clipped and very distant.

"Oh . . ." I stumbled, "what do I call you now?"

"Some of my friends are beginning to call me ma'am," came the reply.

"Ah, well, ma'am, I've just received some copies of the book with your profile in it and wondered if you'd like one . . . I can always drop it in at the Mews."

"No. Don't do that. Come to lunch. What about next Thursday?"

"Wonderful. See you then."

Of course, I never did. Lunch was canceled by a lady-in-waiting some days later. I quite understood. Not only had Sarah undergone the great Mysterium Coniunctionis (the mystical wedding), but the fact that she was now royal by marriage meant she had to be very careful with whom she mixed.

Which brings us to Steve Wyatt and John Bryan. To give Sarah her due, her heart is a far more motivating force than her cerebellum. There is no doubt that she suffered greatly from Andrew's long absences at sea. A marriage needs a lot of work—and more important, a lot of continuity—especially in the early stages.

And with Sarah's deep insecurity and Andrew's inability to provide her with enough reassurances, it was only a matter of time before she began to look outside her marriage to supply what was lacking within it. Steve Wyatt may be credited with being the first Texan to captivate Sarah, but the more enduring relationship turned out to be with his friend and colleague, fellow Texan John Bryan.

The extent of Bryan's romantic connection with Sarah did not become apparent until August of 1992, when *Paris Match,* and subsequently the *Daily Mirror,* published pages of photographs of the two lovers by the poolside of a remote villa in the south of France. Although Sarah was separated from Andrew at this time, her relationship with Bryan had been upheld as purely a professional one. John Bryan was her "financial advisor." And since he was also a friend of Andrew's, he had played a key role earlier in the year trying to effect a reconciliation between the Yorks.

The publication of these intimate photographs was acutely embarrassing to the royal family, and coupled with the Diana Squidgy tapes (see Chapter VII) a mere few days later, dealt a mortal blow to the monarchy. However, this major humiliation for both Sarah and the royal family did not bring about the collapse of her relationship with Bryan. The couple continued to be seen together socially throughout 1993 and beyond. Yet it's difficult to fathom quite why she and Johnny Bryan have managed to extract such a durable relationship out of so few astrological connections. Admittedly, with no accurate birth time, vital pieces of the astrological jigsaw are missing, but nonetheless, as a strongly Cancerian man, Bryan does not seem to reflect the Mars-Superman etched in Sarah's chart. And with his Venus in Gemini, it's difficult to see where Sarah fits in. The archetypes simply aren't being mirrored.

Which leads me to believe that Sarah has still not found Mr. Right. But could Steve Wyatt have been Mr. Right? Wyatt represented all manner of attractions for Sarah. Compared to Andrew, who had become something of a couch potato when not on board ship, Wyatt was the epitome of fun, sophistication, and hedonism. He was also much taken with New Age philosophies. And he was very good-looking indeed. But lacking any reliable birth data, it is impossible to make any judgments as to whether he was truly right for Sarah. What is very clear in the astrology, however, is that at the time of her association with Wyatt, Sarah was experiencing the sort of

transits that would evoke a deep longing to be passion-
ately transformed by love. And in much the same way
as Sarah just happened to come along at the astrological moment Andrew was primed to fall in love, Steve
Wyatt was the catalyst for Sarah's transformation.
And it certainly gave her a taste for America and all
that the United States holds in the way of freedom and
lack of red tape.

Asked by *Today* to write an astrological perspective
on the relationship between Wyatt and Sarah and the
future of the Yorks' marriage, I was able to say in
March of 1992:

> *Andrew, with several planets in stoical Capri-*
> *corn, can no doubt cope with a lack of continuity*
> *in his marriage, but Sarah, with her Scorpio-*
> *rising insecurity, cannot. Distance for her does*
> *not lend enchantment but frustration and depres-*
> *sion. As soon as Pluto began to nudge her rela-*
> *tionship axis in 1990 and 1991, if she was in any*
> *way feeling neglected and lonely within her mar-*
> *riage, she would be vulnerable to love and affec-*
> *tion outside it.*
>
> *Enter Mr. Steve Wyatt.*
>
> *Mr. Wyatt is the personification of Venus-Libra*
> *at its oily best—smoothness and charm ooze*
> *from every pore as if from a pool the size of a*
> *Texas oil field . . .*
>
> *The Duke and Duchess of York, like the Prince*
> *and Princess of Wales, are, to many people,*
> *idealized models of modern marriages. Thus, it*

matters tremendously how they respond—or are seen to respond—to crisis situations. Clearly Andrew and Sarah have been knocked sideways by the recent revelations, and there is no question that this has put extra strain on an already delicate state of affairs . . .

Although, astrologically speaking, their marriage is by no means made in heaven, Andrew and Sarah may well have enough love to bridge the recent gulf between them. But unless they use Pluto's transformational influence now, when revolutionary Uranus contacts both their charts in 1994/95, it may all be over but the shouting.

At the time Andrew met Sarah, his chart was redolent with images of marriage. He had the classic astrological pointers for marriage—progressed Venus conjunct his sun in the seventh house of love and relationships, and the progressed Descendant also conjunct the sun. It was akin to the enchanted Titania in *Midsummer Night's Dream* falling in love with the first person she met on waking—the donkey-headed Bottom. I'm not suggesting here that there was anything remotely asinine about Andrew falling in love with Sarah, but it was the right time for him, and Sarah arrived on the scene on cue—whether or not they would still seem made for each other when the love potion had worn off.

Andrew, like Charles, is not used to the real world of women. It is to his credit that he fell in love with Koo Stark, who may not have had the right royal credentials, but she did have perfect astrological ones, and she certainly provided an anchor for Andrew's Piscean temperament. Andrew is not an easy man to be with. Uranus is conjunct his Ascendant in regal Leo, which makes him very volatile, arrogant, and difficult. He wants his own way, and even though he is a sentimental and pliable Pisces, he's been brought up in a setting wherein he can click his fingers and everyone, especially women, come running. Sarah, of course, isn't like that. She's her own woman and likes her own way, too. Both would have put up a pretty good show of giving in to each other in the early stages of their relationship, but given enough hostilities and too few opportunities to kiss and make up, ice and frost would soon put out any passionate sparks.

Andrew's ideal woman must have plenty of earth in her chart. Capricorn, Taurus, or Virgo should figure, either by sun sign, Venus, Moon, or Ascendant. Sarah is distinctly lacking in earth. And for her part, she has no indications of wanting a Pisces-Neptune man to hitch her wagon to: She wants an Aries action man, a Taurean or a Libran. As it was, a combination of all these astrological lacks, the difference in where they were each coming from, and the enforced separations guaranteed the marriage a short life. However, it must be said that throughout their troubles and right up to the present day, Andrew has loyally and lovingly supported Sarah and they remain good friends.

The shocking revelation in January of 1992 that Sarah had been on holiday with a man who was not her husband was the first shot across the bows in what turned out to be for the Queen, and certainly for Charles, Diana, Andrew, and Sarah, an "annus horribilis." And it wasn't exactly an "annus felicitus" for me either. Three weeks after the discovery of the photographs, I joined *Today* newspaper as its astrologer. This appointment had come about in a somewhat fateful way. In November of 1991, there was a small party to launch my book *Divine Encounters*. The venue was Gascognes, a wine bar in St. John's Wood, and, although it was a private party, the restaurant was still open to customers. In fact, they had to walk through the book gathering in order to get to the bar. Making his way to have a quiet drink after a disappointing day, Charles McCutcheon picked up a copy of *Divine Encounters* and glanced through it while he sat at the bar. On his way out, he took me to one side, introduced himself, and suggested it might make the basis of a series of six plays and asked me to ring him. Two weeks later, he was negotiating my contract with his close friend Martin Dunn, the editor of *Today* newspaper.

My encounter with Charles may not have been exactly divine, but it was certainly destined. During the course of the next six weeks, Charles became my manager and a confidant in the truest sense of the word. He had opened the door to a lucrative career for me, and I was immensely grateful and trusting of him. Sometime in January I told him of my association with the Princess of Wales, because I knew a book by

Lady Colin Campbell was coming out in the spring and that it would disclose my link with Diana. And I thought he was someone who should know. Charles, on the other hand, believed that Martin Dunn should also be told. After all, he explained, it would be a gross slap in the face at the very least not to tell the person who would need to have his finger on the button of such a sensational story. It would also appear to be a betrayal of trust if I wasn't prepared to give my employers an advance warning. I agreed to tell Martin, but only on condition that the contract had already been struck and signed. Therefore, at the end of January, over lunch in the Camden Brasserie, with the encouraging presence of Charles, I reluctantly told Martin. It would be the understatement of the year to say his reaction was one of pleasant surprise. Gobsmacked is probably a little nearer the mark.

Then on March 22—ironically, my birthday—an article in the *Sunday People* reported almost verbatim a conversation I had had with Diana on March 9. During our early March conversation, we had discussed the publication of Colin Campbell's book and the fact that it would reveal my six-year association with Diana. Diana gave me her reassurances that she understood my position and that she attributed no blame to me. She already knew full well of the existence of the book and she added that the family was preparing to "batten down the hatches." It turned out to be the last conversation we ever had. The article, published in the *People* on March 22 bearing the byline of Tina Weaver, was written in such a way that it made me out to be the soul of indiscretion. The story, under the banner headline THIS ILL-STARRED ROYAL LOVE, began,

> *Princess Diana confided to a top* People's *stargazer two months ago that the marriage of the Duke and Duchess of York was doomed . . . From her experience of doing readings for the Duchess, she believes her marital troubles stem from "an excessive need for love." Blond Penny told a male pal: "She is very insecure. The more she demanded attention from Andrew, the more he held back . . . Just three weeks ago Di phoned Penny at her lakeside home in Hampshire because she was worried about the contents of a new book by society hostess Lady Colin Campbell. "The Princess was bracing herself for the worst," Penny told the friend. The astrologer also revealed that all has not been rosy between the royal sisters-in-law. "But they have now smoothed things over," said Penny's friend. "The Princess has even told Penny that she is deeply concerned about the future of the monarchy and that she is intent on doing her best to preserve its image . . ."*

Horror-struck, I read the article realizing that Diana would be in no doubt, given the authenticity of the reported conversation, that I had indeed broken her trust—blabbed to a "male friend" who had clearly sold the story for a sum of money. I wrote to her immediately, posting the letter the following day, Monday, March 23.

Dear Diana,

If it's not one thing, it seems to be another. On top of all the hoo-ha [the news of the Yorks' separation], now you have the worry of your father [Earl Spencer had just been taken seriously ill]. I'm so sorry and hope that it won't be too long before he is on the mend.

As you can imagine, I'm writing to you because of the article in the People. *It came as the most tremendous shock to me—just as I got home yesterday from a birthday lunch with my family. There was a message on the Ansaphone from my mother-in-law. I was absolutely horrified. Why, after six years, does this suddenly come out now?*

I have thought about it long and hard. My husband was the only witness to the phone call, so either he inadvertently informed a friend of his or the phone lines are bugged . . . The second alternative, that the information has come from those who monitor such calls, raises the issue of why. The motive? I can only assume it's to put me in as dubious a light as possible prior to the publication of L.C.C.'s book.

Anyway, I am devastated because it seems as though I have totally broken the trust between us. All I can do is assure you I have had no part whatsoever in this article. I am deeply sorry about the whole mess and hope desperately that it has caused you little embarrassment—especially at this traumatic time.

Upon reading the *People* article on that Sunday in March, I reread the notes of my conversation with Diana on the ninth. Certainly we had discussed the monarchy and her desire to "do her best for its image," and we had also discussed all of the issues raised in the article. But during our exchange Diana had also informed me, in regard to the Yorks' marriage, that "Sarah was about to do something very dramatic." Implicit in the remark was that the demise of the Yorks' marriage was about to be made official. Strangely enough, this part of the telephone conversation was not mentioned in the *Sunday People* article. What I was not aware of at the time was that on Sunday, March 8, the day before Diana's phone call, the Queen had made a last-ditch attempt to save Sarah and Andrew's marriage. She had driven over to the Yorks' home in Sunninghill, Romenda Lodge, for tea, but although there was considerable sympathy, there was no change of heart. Some ten days later, on March 18, the *Daily Mail*'s front page announced: AN-DREW AND FERGY TO PART.

What also never entered my head until the extraordinary developments of 1993 was that Diana could have quite deliberately given me the information of the Yorks' imminent separation, if only to see what I might do with it—a test of loyalty, if you like.

By some strange quirk of fate, the separation an-

nouncement coincided with the third day of the
serialization in the *Sun* newspaper of Lady Colin
Campbell's book, *Diana in Private.* Monday and
Tuesday had covered various aspects of Diana's char-
acter previously unknown, even undreamed-of.
Wednesday's extract was to cover my meeting with
Diana in 1986. As luck would have it, the story never
emerged. The Yorks' separation totally eclipsed the
Colin Campbell revelations, and were it not for An-
drew Morton, few people would ever have got to know
Diana had consulted an astrologer—at least this
astrologer.

And although I was relieved that a storm of controversy did not arise, *Today* was disappointed, to say the
least, that they could not lay claim to having "Princess
Di's astrologer" on the paper. However, when *Diana
in Private* was actually launched on Friday, April 3,
the information was "out on the streets" and Martin
Dunn, as an astute and ambitious tabloid editor, quite
naturally wanted to make the most of it.

I had lunch at Bibendum on that Friday with my
manager, Charles, and an American journalist,
"Alan." Alan had been a good friend for several years,
and since he had been invited to the publication party
for *Diana in Private,* he came to the table clutching a
copy. Although I had spoken briefly to Lady Colin
Campbell in the summer of 1991, when she telephoned asking me to corroborate her information that
Diana had consulted me, I had no idea what would
appear on the printed page. What needs to be set
straight for the record here, however, is the reason

why Lady Colin Campbell's rendition of the astrological content was so accurate.

Lady Colin Campbell's phone call to me in the summer came as a bolt from the blue. Here was a woman confronting me with a string of facts that no other journalist had ever unearthed. Her information, she assured me, had come from a source "close to the Princess." As she continued to speak to me, I began to realize that I had very definitely heard that unusual singsong voice before.

"Excuse me," I said, "but I have a feeling I know you. You aren't Georgie Zadie, are you?"

"Yes, I am," came the astonished reply.

"Well, it's me, Penny—Bina Gardens Penny."

Back in the mid-seventies, I had spent three months in a flat owned by Jan Powell in Bina Gardens, South Kensington. Also staying there for a short time was Georgie. And although we got on well during our time at the flat, we had not kept up the friendship. It was simply one of those extraordinary coincidences. During that phone call, we relived past times and past acquaintances, so by the end of our conversation, it seemed somewhat churlish not to tell her she was at least on the right track. When, eventually, I was contacted by the *Sunday Express,* who originally held the serialization rights for *Diana in Private,* I immediately informed Diana of what had taken place. And I was given firm reassurances that all was well.

Later, on Friday, April 3, the day *Diana in Private* was launched, Charles and I went to the *Today* offices in Fortress Wapping, the home of Rupert Murdoch's newspaper group, News International. The idea being that Martin, Charles, and I would sit down and discuss a strategy regarding what had come to be called the "Diana business." But instead of meeting Martin, I was confronted by a female journalist with a tape recorder and asked, "On that first meeting with Diana, what was the sitting room like?"

When it became clear I had no intention of adding to Lady Colin Campbell's version of events, the situation went rapidly downhill. The journalist switched off her tape recorder and left. Martin arrived moments later. He was icy, and the concept that I would be committing professional suicide by discussing intimate details of my meetings with Diana cut no ice at all. At one point in our conversation, I threatened to break my contract if there had been any covert agreement that my position as *Today*'s astrologer rested on my association with Diana. Both Charles and Martin dismissed the notion out of hand. After an unbearably difficult quarter of an hour, Martin left the office, handing the situation over to the features editor, David Nicholson. And it was thanks to the combined efforts of David and Charles that the policy of "making a virtue of discretion" was born. The following Monday, a muted article on page five of *Today,* penned by Chris Hutchins, quoted only from the Campbell book. There were no comments by me at all.

Martin never forgave me for not giving *Today* the exclusive he believed was "theirs" by right. He considered my lack of cooperation a flagrant breach of personal trust and utter disloyalty to the newspaper who paid my salary and gave me a prominence I would not otherwise have had. As David Nicholson was later to say to me, "We can take anyone off the streets and make them into a star. And we can break them just as easily."

But while there was a minor war of words and wills taking place between the powers that be at *Today* and myself, a rather different form of battle, perhaps more of a crusade, appeared to be taking place in the Mirror group. On April 19 yet another embarrassing article graced the pages of the *Sunday People.* In a small box, juxtaposed between a piece on the Yorkshire Ripper (Tina Weaver again) and another on Liz Taylor, was a small article headed DI'S MARRIAGE MENDER FACES DI-VORCE NO. 2. This story claimed that my own marriage had broken down entirely because of my relationship with another man. Unfortunately, in light of future events, whoever had provided the newspaper with the story in the first place named the man involved, "fellow astrologer Felix Lyle."

It would turn out to be yet another twist in a tale of a thousand subplots.

To my relief at the time, no one in the media thought the idea of Diana's "marriage mender" having her own tangled mess particularly newsworthy and the story died on the pages of the *People.* That is, at least until there was suddenly a cause to resurrect it some three months later. That cause, by great irony, was provided by Andrew Morton.

On June 7, the serialization of Morton's book,

Diana, Her True Story, began in the *Sunday Times.* The first extract contained details of Diana's purported suicide attempts, her battle with bulimia, and that she had sought astrological advice from me. This first extract caused a proverbial sensation and all the newspapers featured Morton's revelations, including the astrological factor, the following day.

A week or so later I received a phone call from Chris Hutchins at *Today.*

"Penny, do you know of an astrologer called Felix Lyle?"

"I do, as it happens . . . Why?"

"Well, according to Andrew Morton's book, he's Diana's astrologer."

Of all the astrologers in all the world to have also been consulted by Diana, it turned out to be the man with whom I had had a devastating love affair some two years beforehand. It did not take long for the rest of Fleet Street to fall upon this extraordinary coincidence. All journalists have access to any copy that has been written about anyone. So when the name Felix Lyle cropped up, "Di's Marriage Mender Faces Divorce No. 2" also cropped up. Now, the media had got used to the idea that Diana had consulted Penny Thornton—and for some years. So it was somewhat of an anomaly to discover that she had consulted another astrologer. Why would Diana change her allegiance from someone who had apparently helped her so much? So, somehow, two and two had to be seen to make four. Both the *Daily Mail* and London's *Evening Standard* came to the conclusion that I must have handed over the mantle to Felix myself. He was my "second-in-command," my acolyte! Of course, it was nothing like that. Felix had known Andrew Morton for some years. They moved in a similar circle which included the Colhursts—James, by marriage, is related to the Princess of Wales—so it was not unnatural that at Morton's or the Colhursts' suggestion, Felix should be put forward to Diana as someone who could also help her.

Needless to say, the irony of the situation did not escape *Today*. And, as Chris Hutchins was to tell me later, when he informed Martin Dunn of Felix's existence and the role he had played in my life, Martin gave a huge guffaw and commented, "So she's human after all . . ."

Perhaps an innocent abroad would have been more to the point.

VII

1992 and All That . . .

Her Majesty the Queen, in a speech delivered at a Guildhall lunch on Tuesday, November 24, summed up 1992 as an "annus horribilis." It was a year that began in a blaze of publicity over the Duchess of York and ended with a fire that decimated part of Windsor Castle. Not a month went by without some revelation about the family splattered across the front pages of all the newspapers.

On March 29, within days of the announcement of the Duke and Duchess of York's separation, while Diana was in Lech, Austria, enjoying a skiing holiday with Charles, William, and Harry, Earl Spencer, Diana's father, suffered a heart attack and died. He had been taken ill a week or so before but had seemed sufficiently well for Diana to leave for a holiday. His sudden death was therefore a double blow for Diana: Not only had she lost her father, but she was a thousand miles away at the time.

I wrote to her immediately:

Dear Diana,

What desperately sad news. I'm so sorry. You must be devastated. The one thing to remember is that he knew how much you loved him, and whatever differences there may have been— and there always are in all families—he would have died knowing that he was loved, whether you were right beside him or a thousand miles away.

As soon as I heard he'd been rushed to hospital, I thought to myself: Oh dear, this is it. Do you remember the birthday "forecast" I sent you? There was a small sentence about your family (Spencer) and something about some glorious happy moments as well as some sadness . . . if a new order enters your life, something must pass away? . . . But, even if some part of you is prepared for a death, the actual event is always a shock.

In many ways, it was marvelous that he had all those extra years and also good that he died so peacefully. In Eastern traditions, it is always thought to be a blessing to drift peacefully away from the body. I'm also sure that his death will coincide with some kind of "birth" for you:

*not a baby, but something in the way of a re-
newal.*

*My condolences to your family and all my love
and thoughts to you.*

The day following her father's death, Diana returned with Charles to London. And the newspapers
took the opportunity to enforce the idea that the two
had become united through the crisis.

Chris Hutchins writing in *Today* was one of many
journalistic voices singing the same ballad.

*In her terrible sadness, Diana has found
Charles to be a pillar of strength. She called to
him from her hotel balcony as soon as she heard
her father had died. His was the shoulder she
cried on . . . The affection of the royal couple was
obvious after they emerged from the Arlberg
Hotel yesterday. Charles clasped her hand com-
fortingly in the car as they were driven to the
airport . . . One of the royal party said,
". . . everyone watching the royal couple felt they
were closer than for a very long time . . . Before
this happened the way they behaved with each
other, stood with each other, seemed to say that
things were much better between them, that a
happier understanding had been restored.*

But Andrew Morton paints a very different view of
what was really taking place at that time, and knowing
full well the sonic depths Diana and Charles's rela-

tionship had really sunk to, I can only agree with his version of events. According to Morton, the united front was nothing more than a media exercise. Diana felt deeply aggrieved that Charles should be allowed to present the image of a caring and supportive husband when for years he had been anything but. However, Diana bowed under pressure from the Queen and conceded that Charles should fly back with her to London.

At the airport, they were duly met by the assembled media, who reported the fact that Charles was lending his support at Diana's hour of need. The reality was that as soon as the royal couple arrived at Kensington Palace, Prince Charles drove immediately to Highgrove, leaving Diana to grieve alone. Two days later Diana drove to the funeral while Charles flew in by helicopter. The friend to whom Diana related this story commented: "He only flew home with her for the sake of his public image. She felt that at a time when she was grieving the death of her father, she could at least be given the opportunity to behave in the way she wanted rather than go through this masquerade.

But it was the last time Diana went along with any attempt to present a united front to the public. And by the time the serialization in the *Sunday Times* of the Morton book began, any vague hopes that the Prince and Princess of Wales liked each other, let alone loved each other, had evaporated into the mists of Avalon, where, indeed, they had come from in the first place. It would be an understatement to say *Diana, Her True Story* generated a huge wave of sympathy and support for Diana. It was a tidal wave of Krakatoan proportions. Charles was cast in the role of the cruel husband and almost universally vilified for cheating on one of the most beautiful and adored women in the world. Conversely, Diana's struggle with bulimia drew her to the hearts of millions of fellow sufferers. And alternative therapies gained a whole new and approving audience overnight.

Aspects of Diana's plight, the reverberations through the royal family, and comments by those involved in the almost surreal drama that developed by the day dominated the front pages of the world's newspapers for the entire month of June. Headlines ranged from WE WON'T DIVORCE (the *Sun,* June 8) to DIANA WANTS OFFICIAL SPLIT (the *Sun,* June 27), I'LL NEVER BE QUEEN (*Today,* June 6) to WE DIVORCE TOGETHER! (*Mail on Sunday,* June 7). This latter article, written by Iain Walker, suggested that the Princess of Wales and the Duchess of York "had a private pact to leave their husbands at the same time . . . But at the last minute, Diana put duty and her children before her own happiness." But however differing the views of the future prospects for the royal couple, the one constant was the rock-solid bank of support from both the media and the public for Diana.

By July a countermovement launched by friends and supporters of Prince Charles was surfacing, but faced with such overwhelming odds in Diana's favor, the enterprise was effectively strangled at birth. Penny Junor did her best to right the balance in *Today* (July 6) with a seven-page spread entitled "Charles: His True Story." According to Junor, there had been "a conspiracy to blacken the name of the heir to the throne." Included was a list of claims made in the Morton book, and Junor was able to refute each and every one. In discussing Camilla Parker Bowles, Junor stated, "[She] has helped him to maintain his sanity in the traumatic marriage. They are very close but are nothing other than very good friends. It is Diana's obsession that makes it sound otherwise . . ." But however wrong Junor may have been about the nature of the relationship between Charles and Camilla, her conspiracy theory has a distinct ring of truth.

It [the conspiracy] *began exactly two years before the publication of the Morton book. Morton was researching a book on Highgrove and the lifestyle of Charles and Diana. At the time Diana was unburdening herself to her closest friends . . . To his surprise, Morton was approached about Charles and Camilla . . . Morton was asked if he could place stories in national papers concerning the time Charles spent with Camilla, especially during his trips across country from Highgrove to the Parker Bowles home at Corsham, Wiltshire, just twelve miles away. Some newspapers were asked to "stake out" the houses and get pictures of the couple. Morton was told pictures might force Charles to break up the friendship or, at least, spend more time with his wife and sons.*

Junor goes on to explain that Diana's friends, urged on by ever more desperate pleas of help from her, not only felt a moral obligation to bring to light Diana's plight, but in order to validate Morton's claims in his book which told her side of the story, they were only too prepared to give media interviews after publication of the book.

They could not have foreseen the international furor that they unleashed. Charles didn't. He was not aware of the conspiracy in any way until the hype for the book indicated Diana was involved.

Even without any knowledge and understanding of the royal family, or more specifically, the strained relationships between Diana and the Queen, Prince Philip, and the Queen Mother, it was clear that behind palace walls Diana was experiencing considerable fallout from the publication of the book. Effectively the family had been plunged into its biggest crisis since the abdication of 1936. And the blame fell on Diana.

According to the *Daily Mail* of June 8:

A senior palace source said: "It has been decided that the royal couple will not be split by this book. They will survive it. The marriage will go on, and that's that. Such sentiments would not be expressed without the knowledge of the Queen. She is nevertheless extremely concerned over the events of this weekend and the devastatingly sharp spotlight which has been focused on her son's marriage, now publicly seen to be an empty shell . . .

All last week, officials were trying to persuade the Princess that a statement should be issued on her behalf distancing her from the two books which have focused on the critical state of unhappiness in her marriage . . . It is suggested that the Morton book . . . was unofficially authorized by Diana.

It is this suggestion, hinted at by publisher Michael O'Mara and tacitly underlined by the Sunday Times *and its editor, Andrew Neil, which infuriated family members and palace officials.*

But despite a series of firm suggestions that it would be in everyone's interests to endorse a statement, the Princess of Wales refused to do so. She has told the palace that she was not in any way connected with the book and cannot be held responsible for what her friends have decided to do off their own bat.

Palace officials were thus able to deny officially that there was cooperation with Andrew Morton on his book. But they did not put Princess Diana's name to the denial, though they would clearly have liked to do so . . .

Whether Diana took an active or passive role in supplying information for Andrew Morton's book may still be a subject of speculation, but the evidence certainly appears to point that way. And Junor's mention of a conspiracy theory gathers even more credence given Lady Colin Campbell's comments to me. Colin Campbell maintains that in October of 1991, while she was working on *Diana in Private,* she was approached on more than one occasion by friends of the Princess to see if she might include some hitherto unknown material on Charles. Campbell remained firm in her intention not to "rubbish Charles." And eventually the overtures ceased. And much, much later, *Diana, Her True Story* did the deed very effectively.

In the wake of the publication of Morton's book, Diana gave every indication that she supported the friends who had spoken out on her behalf. Telephone calls were made to certain newspapers to alert them in advance that she would be visiting a particular friend mentioned in the book. The following day, photographs would dutifully appear showing her embracing the friend affectionately. In standing by them she gave clear nonverbal signals that the stories contained in the book were authentic. However, when it became increasingly clear that there was a growing chorus of disapproval over her apparent condonation of a book declaring her husband, the heir to the throne, to be an uncaring father, her tactics appeared to change. Suddenly James Gilby, one of her closest and most loyal friends, became persona non grata. As, indeed, did massage therapist Stephen Twigg. According to the *Sunday Express* on July 12,

SAD DIANA DROPS THE ROYAL MOLE

Princess Diana has abruptly severed contact with James Gilby, the man who claimed she attempted suicide five times. He is no longer welcome at her royal residences and has been struck off the privileged list of people given swift and direct access to the Princess. His name was suddenly removed last month during the controversy over Andrew Morton's biography: Diana: Her True Story. *It is now believed Diana gave tacit approval for the book. But following the dismissal of her masseur, Stephen Twigg, and the dropping of Gilby, it seems that she is trying to distance herself from it . . .*

I was not so publicly dumped, but silence hath a mighty sound, and the fact that Diana had not contacted me for over three months made it clear that our relationship had been terminated. I understood and was not surprised. Just a little hurt.

Nevertheless, at that time I still felt tremendous affection for Diana, so that when an article in *Today* with my byline stated, "The second eclipse . . . occurs on June 30 in the sign of Cancer and could mark a major upset in the life of the Princess of Wales" — words I had not written myself — I felt bounden to explain matters. She really did not need her ex-astrologer adding to the general climate of catastrophe. TV footage and countless photographs were revealing a distraught Diana clearly buckling under the weight of the controversy raging all about her, and my heart went out to her.

Dear Diana,

I had to write because I couldn't stand on the sidelines any longer . . . The reason I haven't written before is that I had assumed you had "struck me off." And maybe you have. But even so, no one could let someone they knew, and someone they cared about, go through all this without a word of support.

God knows how you're surviving the pressure—although perhaps now so much of the internal (family) battle is being externalized, in a strange way it's better . . .

I have enclosed the original article I had written for Today *so that you will have a better idea what I was getting at. I'm sorry about the headline that fronted it* (DIANA: SET FOR AN ECLIPSE OF THE HEART)*, but that choice rests with the newspaper. The one I had chosen was "Eclipse? What eclipse?" And also the bit about your facing a major upset was not written by me.*

I'm also sorry about your photograph appearing above the stars column. [Since the publication of *Diana in Private,* a headshot of Diana had appeared alongside mine in the newspaper.] *It has gone now, but the acknowledgment (Astrol-*

WITH LOVE FROM DIANA

*oger to Princess Diana) is still there, I'm afraid.
Nothing I can do about it . . .*

*Anyway, the important thing is that whatever
your opinion of me, I had to let you know that I
am thinking of you so very much. And even if you
shred this on arrival, knowing that I sent it is
important for me.*

*Take great care . . . be strong: Know that you
are standing in your own truth, and when this
happens you are impregnable and unassailable.*

While at first the pendulum had swung very much
in Diana's favor, bit by bit, doubts began to be raised
in various quarters not only at the wisdom of her
apparent collaboration with Morton, but what had
been the real motivation. Was it simply to wake up the
world in general, and Charles in particular, to her
immense problems and injustices? Or was it a pre-
emptive strike? A desperate measure to have the facts
from her side presented to the world in the event of a
scandal breaking that would put her in a bad light.

On Sunday, March 22, the *News of the World* was
intending to publish photographs, allegedly taken by a
stableboy, of the Princess and James Hewitt. The
pictures were by no means indecorous, but they
revealed a certain intimacy. However, since Diana's
father had just been rushed to the hospital and in
respect of her feelings, the *News of the World* made a
decision not to print them.

It might not be such a gross assumption therefore to

suggest that Diana knew full well something faintly scandalous was going to emerge at some point during the year, and in order to preempt a fall from grace, or at least cushion her from a severe dent to her image, she would need to set the stage in the most understanding light possible.

But while the photographs remained under wraps, it seemed a tape recording could not.

I had been in Portugal on holiday with my children for only two days when Charles McCutcheon rang to tell me of the publication of the Sarah and Bryan photographs. Before I had time to even go a gentle biscuit color, the Squidgy Tapes had hit the headlines.

On Monday, August 24, the *Sun* published a transcript of a telephone call allegedly between the Princess of Wales and a "mystery man"—later identified as James Gilby. The telephone call was deemed to have been made on New Year's Eve 1989. The exchange of information and feelings was such that there was little question that the two were lovers.

HIM: Did you go to church today?

HER: Yes, I did.

HIM: Did you, Squidge?

HER: Yes.

HIM: Did you say lots of prayers?

HER: Of course.

HIM: Did you? Kiss me, darling (sound of kisses being blown down the phone).

HER: (sound of laughter and returns the kisses) . . .

And there was more. Only the *Sun* wisely decided to censor the transcript, and when a telephone line was set up by Broadsystems, News International's telecommunication company, so that the public could dial in and listen to the tape, this, too, was edited. But since I record *Today*'s horoscope phone lines at Broadsystems, on my return from Portugal I was able to hear the unexpurgated version for myself. At the time, there was considerable speculation as to whether the tape was an outright forgery or the genuine article. But having had many conversations over the years with Diana myself, there was absolutely no question in my mind as to the authenticity of the female voice. It was Diana.

There was also no question over the disastrous effect this tape had on Diana's image. Diana had emerged from the Morton book a combination of Mother Teresa and Helen of Troy—and, perhaps less laudably, as Diana the Martyr. Now the public had to deal with the very real possibility that she was as unfaithful to her husband as he had apparently been to her. The Princess was wobbling on her pedestal. However, she did not fall off. The Morton book had successfully done its bit to create a bedrock of understanding for just such an eventuality.

After the initial intense speculation over the future of the Waleses' marriage generated in June by *Diana, Her True Story,* rumors of an impending separation died down. The palace policy of rising above the situation and refusing to comment on it was put into being. As in times past, it was believed, if a situation was not publicly acknowledged, it would simply fade away. However, in August the Squidgy Tapes brought it back with a vengeance. And with the close proximity of this event to the Sarah and Bryan photographs, there cannot be many people who didn't suspect some stage management had been involved.

Indeed, the tape the *Sun* transcribed was not the only tape of this New Year's Eve telephone call. There had been at least two transmissions of the same tape: one recorded by a secretary, Jane Norgrove, on the New Year's Eve in question, and another by a man called Cyril Reenan—mysteriously recorded on January 4, 1990, some four days later. Furthermore, the tapes had been in the *Sun's* possession since January of 1990. James Gilby had been informed of their existence then and he had presumably warned Diana. And even though the *Sun* apparently only decided to publish the Squidgy Tapes in August of 1992 because America's *National Enquirer* had "pipped them to the post," it still begs the question, whose hand was on the release button in the first place?

The taping of royal telephone calls could provide enough material for an entire book, but one intriguing aspect of the whole subject is worthy of mention here. On December 29, 1986, while experimenting with a scanning device in Highgate, London, Paul (see Chapter VI) and his girlfriend Vicky picked up a conversation between a young woman and an older man. Clearly affected by the woman's desperate plea to speak at length to the man, he agreed to stop his

Range Rover at the first opportunity. He was driving west along the Marylebone Road at the time, having just passed Harley Street. Paul and Vicky did not recognize either of the voices at first but were compelled to listen because the woman sounded at her wits' end. She was on the verge of tears. It was only when the man asked where the Queen was and the woman replied—in the next room, playing cards—that they immediately reached for the cassette recorder.

The tape of this telephone call was subject to the same procedure as the Rothermere photographs (see Chapter VI). Detective Constable Tom Reed at Scotland Yard was given the tape immediately, as was the late Trevor Kempson of the *News of the World* (who worked for British intelligence). Since 1984, Paul and Trevor had been endeavoring to bring to public attention the danger mobile phones presented. Conversations were all too easy to pick up with the use of the simplest of scanning devices, which meant that public figures, top businessmen, and the like ran the constant risk of being overheard, therefore making themselves vulnerable to blackmail—and worse. Indeed, this conversation between the Princess of Wales and an unknown man was a case in point.

The tapes, like the alleged photograph of Sarah and the yuppie drug dealer have never surfaced, and Paul himself never kept a copy. But he vividly remembers certain key details. According to him and his girlfriend, Diana talked about William singing the Beatles song "The Yellow Submarine," which he'd learned at nursery school. They also remember an arrangement being made between the man and woman to meet at the flat. The man was deeply concerned that she should not say too much over the phone, and according to Paul, it was the consensus of those who listened to the tape that the man in question was linked to the army. Perhaps most significant of all— and a point that Paul is adamant about—is that the man referred to her as Squidgy: evidence that perhaps more than one person close to Diana used this as a nickname for her.

In late August of 1992 anticipation of a separation announcement mounted. But still no official statement was made. One or two of my friends whose business it was to know future court arrangements insisted that a separation would not take place. Both Diana and Charles had joint commitments well into 1993; therefore, rumors of a parting of the ways were not only exaggerated but clearly not on the royal menu at all. However, I could not ignore the astrological omens. I had stuck my neck out all those years ago and, unless some other quite unexpected disaster was to strike the royal family, I fully expected a separation.

The first weekend of October I was in Norway giving a series of lectures—one of them on the House of Windsor. Discussing the abdication crisis of 1936 and pointing to the similar pattern of eclipses in December of 1992, I reiterated my belief that an announcement of a royal separation was imminent: if not following the weekend of October 11, when a full moon at eighteen degrees of Aries and Libra combined with Uranus and Neptune looked combustible enough to inflame any simmering situation, then on or around December 9, at the time of a total lunar eclipse.

The weekend of October 11 came and went without any significant developments. However, by the time the Waleses' royal visit to Korea was at an end—the first week of November—it was clear that the facade of togetherness was not merely threadbare but nonexistent. You did not need to be an expert on body language to see that this couple was doing its best to inform the world that they were not together. And had no intention of ever being so—even in name only.

But still the denials streamed forth from the palace: No—the couple just need breathing space . . . Then, as Diana and Charles returned from Korea, a fresh set of revelations emerged in Andrew Morton's updated paperback version of *Diana, Her True Story.* Quite the most sensational was the disclosure of an angry exchange of letters between Diana and Prince Philip. But instead of letting speculation die down, Diana contacted the Press Association and issued a fifty-three-word statement that did more to confirm Andrew Morton's assertions over the state of the marriage and the pressures exerted on Diana by the palace than throw cold water over them.

The Princess of Wales would like to single out from the recent wave of misleading reports about the royal family . . . The suggestion that the Queen and the Duke of Edinburgh have been anything other than sympathetic and supportive is untrue and particularly hurtful.

By failing to deny reports of her marriage difficulties while maintaining that the Queen and the Duke had been supportive, she effectively endorsed speculation that the marriage was on the rocks. And that a separation or divorce was not out of the question.

But Diana had only a week or so to wait before fate produced a masterstroke in her favor. On November 13 the *Daily Mirror* revealed the existence of a taped conversation, allegedly between the Prince of Wales and Camilla Parker Bowles. And overnight, Camillagate was born. The full transcript of the telephone conversation that took place on December 18, 1989, had already appeared in Australia, but perhaps because intimate exchanges of the photographic or audio type were becoming almost commonplace, the impact on the British public was slightly less shocking than it might have been. In fact, the general response was one of bemusement. There was something deeply incongruous about the rather repressed public persona of Charles masking a desire to become one of Mrs. Parker Bowles's Tampaxes in another life. But however bizarre some of the longings shared between Camilla and Charles, what was abundantly clear from the tape was that their relationship was an extremely loving and supportive one. And, of course, what it did more than anything else was vindicate Diana and prove Andrew Morton to be 100 percent correct.

It took until December 9—exactly on the solar eclipse—for the announcement to come.

It was around 1:30 P.M. and I was working in my study when David Nicholson from *Today* phoned. "It's happening, Penny . . . John Major is making a statement in the House of Commons at three P.M. this afternoon. They're going for a separation. You have to say something now. We want a couple of thousand words as soon as possible . . ."

While I had refused point-blank earlier in the year to make any comments on Diana, I had promised *Today* that when the couple separated, I would write an article or agree to an interview—the rationale being that since I had stuck my neck out in 1988 and predicted a separation and an ensuing constitutional crisis, it deserved some kind of comment by me when it became a reality. And so on December 15 in the context of an interview with Chris Hutchins, I was to say in regard to what lay ahead in 1993 for the solo Princess:

> *Penny believes that both Diana and Charles have suffered from the breakup of the marriage and that there will be no "winners" in the battles to come. She is certain, however, that the separation will end in divorce.*
>
> *"This time is an enormous test of the health of a woman who is extremely vulnerable to emotional pressures. In many ways it is unfair . . ." [But]*

Penny believes Diana will survive all these crises —because she is a born survivor. "Diana is very good at facing a situation. She isn't someone who seeks refuge in fantasy . . . She can know the worst . . . When the chips are down, Diana is a very tough cookie indeed. She's capable of doing very well in a major crisis. Yes, Cancerians do whinge and whine. It's a temperamental thing. But when the crunch comes, she gets on with it. She's a great survivor. As for these comments that she's an arch manipulator, we can look back on anyone's life and review situations from a certain perspective and see them as manipulative or self-seeking or whatever. But I would say that underneath it all, Diana is a survivor and she will do anything to survive. And I see that as a quality, not a fault.

"1993 is going to be a colossal year for her, and she will need to draw on every positive lesson she has ever learned if she is to get through it."

When the astrology works and can be seen to work, it does more than give one a smug sense of satisfaction. It validates the subject and makes all those years of effort and study worthwhile. It had been obvious to me many years beforehand that by the time Saturn entered Aquarius in 1991 and began to make its way toward a tense angular relationship with Pluto in 1993, thereby touching every sensitive point on the charts of Diana, Charles, the Queen, Andrew, and Sarah—indeed, the entire royal family—the monarchy would be heading for an colossal crisis. And, right on target, on the day of a total solar eclipse at eighteen of Sagittarius—a key degree area for the royal family —the announcement was made of the Waleses' separation with all its huge implications for the future of the monarchy.

The official acceptance of the demise of the Waleses' marriage came three weeks after perhaps the most distressing event of the Queen's annus horribilis: the catastrophic fire at Windsor Castle. In the midst of constant sniping by the media—which was on this occasion an accurate barometer of public opinion— regarding the failure of the Queen to adapt to the changing times, particularly where her tax situation was concerned, no one could fail to be affected by the sight of her distraught head-scarfed figure standing amid the tangle of fire hoses around the charred shell of her beloved St. George's Chapel. The fire at the very home of the Windsor dynasty was a symbol of much, much more. And this was a theme I took up in my column at the beginning of December.

On October 2 this year, I gave a talk on the British monarchy at an astrological conference in Oslo . . . One of the points I made was that within a matter of a few short weeks, a dramatic event would strike at the heart of the royal family . . .

October's full moon almost certainly marked an internal crisis for the family: The sheer misery on the faces of Charles and Diana in Korea said everything there was to say about the acrimony and fierce argument taking place behind royal walls . . .

But the most dramatic event at which we can point the lunar finger is the fire at Windsor Castle. It is this devastating accident that has brought the monarchy not to its knees but to its senses. In the wake of the outcry over the multimillion-pound restoration bill expected to be footed by we taxpayers, the Queen has brought forward her decision to pay tax.

But this is where we depart from the external realities of the piece and take a look at the more mystical side of things.

The monarchy is not so much a giant soap opera as a mythological drama: The Queen and Prince Philip aren't ordinary mortals; they aren't Mr. and Mrs. Windsor but Zeus and Hera. Accordingly, we have placed them on their Olympian pedestals only to see them tumble because of their human frailty. And now there is a Greek chorus of disapproval. The Greeks had a word for overweening arrogance—or what happens when we mortals believe we are above celestial law—it is hubris.

Whatever insights there are to be gained from the razing to the ground of the House of Windsor—or at least a part of it—the symbolism of the family seat going up in flames cannot have been lost on the monarchy. Given that it has been a year of unparalleled crisis and criticism for Her Majesty, there has been comparatively little acknowledgment on the monarchy's part that it ought to make some adjustments to itself. Repeated shots across her bow via the media were seemingly ignored: It took a disastrous fire to drive the message home. And so, in the spirit of a Greek tragedy, the Windsor family has been made acutely aware of hubris.

On Friday, November 20, at precisely 11:37 A.M., a small spark ignited a curtain that led to the great fire of Windsor—a fire that burned for almost twenty-four hours and left the Queen's favorite chapel a charred skeleton. At precisely 11:37 A.M. on Friday, November 20, the same degree of Capricorn was rising as that of the Queen's birth. Also, the same degree of Scorpio was directly overhead at the time of both events. But on Friday, November 20, 1992, Pluto—a symbol of hubris if ever there was one—was also directly overhead.

We astrologers are used to events having their signature written in the stars, but this particular piece of synchronicity, or serendipity, is quite staggering. Not only was the chart a perfect "picture" of a fire with consequences way beyond any structural damage, but the repetition of the Queen's horoscope made clear that this was an event targeted at the very heart of the monarchy.

Pluto's theme is transformation, and his emblem is the phoenix rising out of the ashes. So Pluto's dominion over this fateful event—his position at the very zenith of the horoscope—is revealing that out of the ashes of destruction a new creation can emerge. And inasmuch as Windsor Castle will be lovingly rebuilt, so, too, will a new order be born as the old monarchical structure passes away.

The royal family is more than a family, more than a great dynasty: It is a lens through which we can glimpse Olympus. For years we have looked up in awe at the life of these rarefied beings. And now we appear to be witnessing the twilight of our demigods. Yet while they may lose their mystique, they also show us the way forward in terms of a very human struggle.

They have served to show us that hubris is not just a Greek myth.

Thus, for the royal family at least, 1992 went out on a suitably tumultuous note. Surely nothing 1993 could produce in the way of scandal, revelation, and contentiousness could possibly eclipse the preceding twelve months . . .

Certainly for me the year began as it intended to go on—in a state of utter Neptunian chaos and confusion. My contract with *Today* had not been quite so simple for my manager, Charles, to negotiate. And reading between the lines, part of the problem was the feeling of the powers that be at *Today* that I had not "delivered the goods" on Diana. However, agreement was eventually reached, and at the beginning of February I began my second term of office with the paper. It had been the opinion of Charles that I should write a book on Diana. He told me he had discussed the idea with *Today* and that "they" would welcome such an endeavor. However, not only did I have serious misgivings about the ethics of launching into print about a client, but writing a daily column (and the supporting twice-weekly horoscope telephone lines) left me barely enough time to read a book, let alone write one. So at the end of January I told him quite flatly that I was not prepared to write a book at that time, although it was not out of the question at some future date. This issue became such a bone of contention between us that eventually we parted company.

But clearly there had been some miscommunication between Charles, myself, and executives of *Today,* because at the end of the month, during a telephone conversation, the features editor, David Nicholson, suddenly asked me how "the book" was progressing. "What book?" came my reply . . . He was obviously surprised, even somewhat concerned, at my response. A matter of days after this exchange, in early March, I was contacted by Nick Campion, a great friend and the ex-astrologer of the *Daily Mail.* He asked me how things were going with *Today* because he had been told by Bernard Fitzwalter that

David Nicholson had been inquiring at his (Bernard's) availability to take over my position. Not surprisingly, this set a small alarm bell going.

During my time at *Today* I had come to know writer and journalist Chris Hutchins quite well. He was an excellent sounding board as well as being warm and very supportive. His advice on this occasion was that I ought to rethink the idea of a Diana book and that the change of heart should be conveyed to certain individuals as soon as possible.

Thus, by the end of March I was able to inform David Nicholson that I had made a start on a royal book and was intending to find a publisher in America.

So imagine my surprise when, some days later on April 8, I was rung by a journalist from the *Express* and asked about the contents of my book on Diana that was about to come out. News certainly travels fast in Fleet Street, I thought. I immediately faxed both Sir Nicholas Lloyd (the editor of the *Daily Express*) and Eve Pollard (the editor of the *Sunday Express*), informing them that I had been contacted by someone claiming to work for the *Express* but that I had not made any comment about the Princess of Wales to him. Nor was I about to have a book on the Princess of Wales published. I added that were any such suggestions "to emerge on the printed page, they would do me incalculable personal and professional damage." And, as a matter of courtesy, I also faxed a copy of these letters to the new editor of *Today,* Richard Stott.

Then, on April 14, I received a letter from David McMaster, the managing editor of *Today,* that was disconcerting to say the least.

Dear Penny,

I was sorry not to have the opportunity to meet you the other week . . . There are indeed many items for discussion, two of which have become urgent matters which I must ask your response on within the week.

I understand from David Nicholson that you have made a start on the book. We are delighted . . .

In our discussions with you [i.e., Charles McCutcheon] *last year, we were given to believe that such a book could be expected by early summer 1993 . . . Is this still your planned publication date? If so, could we please see a synopsis or any of the material that you have written so far . . .*

On a rather more serious matter, the Princess of Wales has personally sent a message to Richard Stott. The basis of the message was to deny any contact with you for several years, indeed from the mid 1980s. She told Richard that she had met you on only one occasion—and that you were not her astrologer.

This places us all in a potentially difficult and acutely embarrassing position, which Richard has instructed me to clarify immediately.

I look forward to an early reply.

I'm not one to panic, but the impression I gained from the letter was that unless I addressed the relevant issues pretty smartly, I might have a small problem of unemployment on my hands. I therefore spoke to my new business manager, David Ravden, immediately, and by the following Friday, April 16, a meeting for the twentieth had been arranged between David McMaster, David Nicholson, David Ravden, and myself, the intention being to iron matters out and clarify everyone's position. It gave me just one week to write a chapter of a book I had not even begun to conceptualize.

One other matter I had to address immediately was Diana. The letter from David McMaster maintained that the Princess herself had made the denial of our association—a factor I found difficult to believe. So I wrote to her on the same day, the fourteenth.

Dear Diana,

I am writing to you because I feel you may not be aware of a certain situation that has developed.

This morning I received a letter from David McMaster at Today *informing me that Richard Stott, the editor, had received a personal message from you denying any association with me—bar one contact in the mid-eighties.*

I can only assume someone is making mischief here. You would never do such a thing, I'm sure, because we both know that simply isn't true. Why on earth would you continue to send Christmas cards and letters, which, of course, I treasure, to someone you only had contact with once and considered of no value? It simply doesn't make sense.

And it also doesn't make sense that you would suddenly act in such a way now. After all, the embarrassing byline "Astrologer to Princess Diana" has been under the column for a year. And, as I mentioned to you in my letter of June 8 last year, I had absolutely no part in the decision to put it there.

So, fundamentally, my letter is to alert you to the possibility that someone is, as I put it, making mischief. Goodness knows why. But perhaps we can both try to sort it out at our respective ends.

I do hope you are well and not finding the stresses and strains of creating a new life for yourself too awful.

I was in David Ravden's office at the time he made the call to David Nicholson to arrange a meeting. In response to the question of proving my association with Diana, David said he had seen photocopies of Diana's letters and cards—the originals of which were in a bank vault—and that if she had indeed claimed that there had only ever been one meeting, then she was clearly lying. And that might be something news-worthy in itself.

Two days later, on April 18, the *News of the World*'s front page story ran:

DI, THE ASTROLOGER AND SECRET LOVE NOTES

> *Princess Diana has fallen out with a stargazer*
> *who advised her over her marriage problems.*
> *Penny Thornton has called herself "Astrologer to*
> *Princes Diana" since last April. Diana admits to*
> *meeting her once for a consultation but has now*
> *officially denied there was any relationship be-*
> *tween them . . . Thornton is furious over Diana's*
> *denial and is writing a book . . . She and her*
> *friends claim Diana is trying to distance herself*
> *from astrology because she is trying to play down*
> *any "cranky" image. The stargazer claims she is*
> *the victim of a palace smear campaign since news*
> *of the book leaked out and she is threatening legal*
> *action that could force Diana to make a court*
> *appearance . . .*

Colorful, but taking Diana to the High Courts was
not exactly on my agenda. However, by then some
sort of book most certainly was. I had become inextri-
cably lodged somewhere between a rock and a hard
place. But by the time of the meeting with all the
Davids on the twentieth, I had completed one chapter
and, for the sake of giving something tangible for the
newspaper to go away with, had created an extract:
Diana will be seen through the eyes of history as one of ◄
the great tragedies of our time. Like all prophets
damned by their own country, her value as a change
bringer, a transformer, cannot be appreciated now.
Her mantle is to drag the monarchy, kicking and

screaming if necessary, at last into the twentieth century.

At that time, in my heart of hearts, I believed that Diana's denial was a story concocted by those with a vested interest in knowing the precise nature of my dialogue with Diana in order to force my hand. I simply could not believe that Diana would do me such an injustice. What simply did not add up was why she had not leapt in and addressed the issue of my not being her astrologer when *Today* newspaper first began to make the claim twelve months before. According to Martin Dunn, in the summer of 1992 the palace had requested that Diana's picture be removed from the top of my column, but there was no complaint about the acknowledgment itself—Astrologer to Princess Diana. Thus by implication the palace had given its endorsement.

The Monday following the *News of the World* "scoop," I contacted Detective Chief Inspector Alex Hall of the Bedfordshire Constabulary and asked him to establish precisely what Diana had or had not done. After all, I had only been told that she had "personally sent a message to Richard Stott." I had no idea whether she had phoned him, faxed him, or met him face-to-face. Later that same day, after speaking with Diana's then police body guard, Ken Warfe, Alex told me: Diana always did and still does consider you her valued friend and confidante—and her astrologer. Alex Hall added, "And that's official. You can quote her. You have permission."

My mind put at rest, I was able to go to the meeting

with *Today* with renewed confidence. Therefore, at lunch on April 20, I showed David McMaster and David Nicholson a photocopy of two handwritten notes from Diana to myself. And by the time the meal had reached its end, it seemed as if the whole business had been settled.

The matter of my contract and the fact that even my then manager, Charles McCutcheon, had not been told himself of my meetings with Diana until the negotiations with *Today* were all but completed has been already discussed in Chapter VI. But mention needs to be made here that there was no clause in my contract stating that my employment rested on my being Diana's astrologer. Neither was a clause to this effect insisted upon in 1993 or 1994 when my contracts were renegotiated.

It wasn't until September of 1993 that I finally discovered the truth of the matter. On March 6, returning from her solo trip to Nepal, Princess Diana walked purposefully into the business class section of the jumbo jet where members of the press who had accompanied her tour were all seated. She made straight for Charles Rae—*Today*'s royal correspondent—and sat beside him. As a great admirer of Diana, he was overwhelmed by being singled out for such special attention and very flattered when she asked him about his family and his work. Just as she was leaving she said: "Oh, by the way, I only ever saw Penny Thornton once—sometime in the mid-eighties. She's never been my astrologer. Perhaps your editor ought to know that."

For a member of the royal family to volunteer information directly to any member of the press—and in view of several witnesses, including James Whitaker, who confirmed the story to me later in the year when we met on a TV program—was unprecedented. The authority of her words could not be doubted. She had to be telling the truth.

I would be a hypocrite were I to deny any sense of being stabbed in the back by Diana, but I did, and still do, understand her reasons. Diana has had to learn how to fight her corner. In order to protect and survive, sometimes she must take an apparently ruthless step. And this was one of them. Either through fears that I would eventually commit to print factors about her life that she would rather keep private or because it had been suggested to her that consulting an astrologer was not in keeping with her image, she needed to discredit me—to eliminate a potential threat to her position and future security. And there are very few people on the planet who, when the chips are down, would not betray someone or something.

The year 1993 proved an immensely challenging one for her. Going it alone, once the separation was an official reality, was never going to be easy, but for much of the time she triumphed. She continued to dominate the front pages of newspapers and magazines, and her popularity seemed undiminished. However, if there was a cold war being conducted between the court of Diana and that of Charles, by the middle of November, she had lost an important battle.

By Charles's forty-fifth birthday on November 14, the writing was on the wall. If he was to have any chance at all of gaining the love and respect of the people, he had to walk out from under Diana's shadow. And that meant she had to go: She had to disappear from the headlines. Thus, on December 3—yes, three days after a lunar eclipse—Diana announced her departure from public life. November 14, Remembrance Sunday, turned out to be her final act of duty representing the royal family.

Astrologically, 1993 was one of the most difficult of recent years for Diana. Saturn and Pluto closed in on the tight configuration involving the moon, Venus, and Uranus. Fears voiced earlier in the year that she might well suffer some kind of physical or mental breakdown would not have been incompatible with such an astrological setup. As it was, she came through. But it was touch and go. She put up a tremendous fight to retain her status, but in the end the Establishment proved more powerful than the individual, even one with such shimmering charisma.

In her short speech to Headway, at London's Hilton Hotel, Diana took the opportunity to make a dramatic and moving departure.

> *A year ago I spoke of my desire to continue with my work unchanged. For the past year I have continued as before. However, life and circumstances alter, and I hope you will forgive me if I use this opportunity to share with you my plans for the future, which now, indeed, have changed.*

When I started my public life twelve years ago, I understood that the media might be interested in what I did. I realized then that their attention would inevitably focus on both our public and private lives but I was not aware of how overwhelming it would become, nor the extent to which it would affect both my public duties and my personal life, in a manner that has been hard to bear. At the end of this year, when I have completed my official engagements, I will be reducing the extent of the public life I have led so far . . .

Diana always had a titanic struggle on her hands trying to retain her royal autonomy. Taking on the Establishment is no Sunday picnic, and unfortunately, Diana's rare and beautiful stone, even when sharpened at the edges, was not enough to slay the Goliath of the royal firm. While the press in good faith followed the line that she herself had made the decision to bow out because of the pressures the media had placed on her, as far as I was concerned, she had clearly been made to do so. Back in the summer in a television interview on the morning of her birthday, I had stated that the combined effect of Saturn and Pluto indicated a power struggle of immense proportions taking place then and in the months to come. And although she put on a marvelous performance of continuing to be able to maintain her high-profile royal status, by the end of the year, she had to relinquish that power.

Nigel Dempster reporting in the *Daily Mail* the day

after her tearful exit from the royal stage authoritatively maintained:

Diana's decision to cut back significantly on public engagements follows what friends describe as "a terrible year during which she has been subjected to the most appalling pressure." The final straw, according to her inner circle, was the sustained criticism, some of it from Buckingham Palace, that she was "stealing the limelight" from her estranged husband whenever they carried out engagements on the same day . . . Her move ends any hopes of a reconciliation with Charles.

Sadly, in the early months of 1994, instead of retreating into comparative obscurity, Diana appeared to take as many opportunities as possible to grab the headlines. And much as the "party faithful" wished her well, there was an increasing feeling that she was hooked on the drug of media attention. Diana, like Margaret Thatcher before her, with her official role taken away, suddenly had nowhere to go. Life was empty.

My own words written on the day of her official departure from the royal stage supply an suitably profound ending, not only to this chapter, but a tempestuous chapter in the history of the royal family.

At 3:20 P.M. on Friday, December 3, the Princess of Wales announced her withdrawal from public life. And while this would come as a tremendous shock to the public, to an astrologer, the

*writing had been on the wall for some consider-
able time. That she had struggled against the combined weight of Saturn, Pluto, and the royal firm
for eleven months—and seemed to be winning—
is a measure of the extraordinary strength of will
she possesses. And immeasurably sad as her
departure must be, for her it is a liberation.*

*At the precise moment she began her speech,
Scorpio was setting. And not just at any point in
this sign, but the all-significant twenty-fifth degree. Not only does this degree figure prominently
in all the charts of the royal family, it was the
self-same degree on the Midheaven of the fire at
Windsor Castle, which was, of course, the
Queen's Midheaven. And since the Queen is the
monarchy, the signature of this moment was well
and truly etched in the stars.*

*Without going into too many technicalities, for
the past eighteen months, Diana's chart has been
a picture of relentless struggle against a force far
stronger than herself. And it was only a question
of time before either her health gave out or she
caved in under pressure from the powers that be.
And with perfect astrological timing, as Mercury,
Saturn, and Pluto combined at twenty-five degrees of Aquarius and Scorpio, push finally came
to shove: A decision was made of immense significance not only for the future of Diana but for
the future of the monarchy. And although the
decision may seem to be the right one in
the circumstances—and certainly the most
expedient—in time to come, the loss of Diana*

from the royal stage will be seen as the call for the last rites for the monarchy.

In her speech, Diana emphasized that "this decision has been reached with the full understanding of the Queen and Prince Philip." And I'm sure they have been endlessly supportive and concerned for Diana's welfare. But given the astrological facts of the piece, there is no question in my mind that Diana has been forced to relinquish her public role—and make no mistake, this is what is happening. Diana's life is her public role, and like a star without a stage, an audience, and a spotlight, she will feel bereft, unwanted, unloved; life will be meaningless.

No, Diana has been backed into a corner and made to see very clearly that she cannot share center stage with her estranged husband. She must disappear and allow his star once more to rise in the Ascendant. While she has consistently banked on her enormous popularity with the public, her glamorous image, and the undying attention of the press, she underestimated the power of the Establishment.

United with Charles, she stood on a pedestal; divided, she fell.

But all is not lost. Diana has attained an almost mythological status with the people. By retreating now, she will, like Greta Garbo and Marilyn Monroe before her, never be forgotten.

She will be immortalized and reign forever as the Queen who never was, Diana the Divine.

VIII

Future: Tense

The King is dead. Long live the republic.

It was a quiet, frosty night. Some would say later, unnaturally quiet. The moon, with its rainbowed aureole, floated high in the cloudless sky and bathed the countryside in a blue-white glow that was at once both beautiful and ghostly. The slate gray Jaguar headed towards the gates of Balmoral—at a purposeful but unrushed speed of forty-five miles per hour. A mile or so behind followed army personnel in an assortment of military vehicles and Land-Rovers. At the exact moment the Jaguar pulled to a halt, some five hundred miles away in St. James's Park, London, a similar lone state car arrived at the gates of Buckingham Palace. And another drew into the forecourt of Kensington Palace. The time was 1:00 A.M. exactly.

The Queen, dressed in her favorite tartan skirt, watched from a window in her sitting room on the first floor of Balmoral Castle. The Duke of Edinburgh stood behind her. Neither spoke. There had been a brief telephone call half an hour earlier warning them of the arrival of the Prime Minister and Colonel Humphrey Palmer on a matter of extreme urgency.

At 1:05 precisely, the Prime Minister and Colonel Palmer were ushered into the library. Twelve minutes later, the Queen, standing in front of the dying embers of the fire in the drawing room, received them. By half past one it was all over. Three hundred and three years of uninterrupted rule by a series of reigning monarchs had come to an end.

Five hundred forty-six miles south, the handover of power had been somewhat less dignified. Some twenty royal Horse Guards, alerted to the situation moments before the arrival of Lieutenant Colonel Gordon Rycart and Sir Arnold Brooks, refused to open the gates. Several shots were fired in the air, waking most of those resident in the palace. In the ensuing panic, fire was exchanged between the Guards and members of the Diplomatic Protection Squad, and two of the Guards were killed.

But by 1:45 the situation had been brought under control. Every route to the palace had been cordoned off. Radio and television stations throughout Great Britain were no longer live on the air but transmitting prerecorded items. Newspaper offices were similarly under a state of siege. As dawn broke, the people of

Great Britain were waking up to the fact that overnight they had become a republic.

If we were to put a date to this hypothetical scenario, some fifteen years from now, perhaps the year 2009, might turn out to be a fitting one. But even if 2009 does turn out to be the year Britain officially becomes a republic, the end of the monarchy will most certainly not come about in such a Hollywoodesque way. Why? Because it is already happening. We are witnessing a silent revolution—a revolution whose most alarming volley of shots was fired in 1992.

I can't be the only person to consider that the scandalous events that dogged the royal family in 1992 were not mere accidents of fate—that it was more than a colossal coincidence that the photographs of John Bryan and the Duchess of York just happened to be taken and released worldwide a matter of days before the Squidgy Tapes hit the headlines. It is almost common knowledge, and certainly well known within the newspaper industry, that the tapes of the telephone calls between the Prince and Princess of Wales and their respective lovers had been given to the *Sun* in early 1990—almost two years before they became public. And, of course, there were other tapes and other photographs mentioned in previous chapters known to have been in the safekeeping of the police since the mid-1980s. And we know from the way Paul (see Chapters VI and VII) liaises with the police and journalists that British intelligence is always aware of situations of a potentially scandalous royal nature.

The taking of the notorious Bryan-Fergie photographs has always been deeply mysterious. How on earth did photographer Daniel Angeli single-handedly manage to get the necessary amount of heavy camera equipment up an impossibly difficult hillside slope in order to capture such remarkable photographs? And who tipped him off in the first place? He almost certainly had to be in situ before the couple arrived, and given some considerable help to remain there and leave incognito. And it doesn't say much for royal security if one or more of their hand-picked detectives was unable to spot a large telephoto lens a mere few meters from the perimeter of a secluded villa.

Chris Hutchins and Peter Thompson make much the same point in their book, *Diana's Nightmare: The Family*. They discuss the fact that two tapes of the Diana/Gilby New Year's Eve conversation were handed over to the *Sun* newspaper—one by secretary Jane Norgrove, recorded on the night in question itself, and the second by Cyril Reenan, mysteriously transmitted some four nights later. One can only deduce that one or both were deliberately transmitted in the hopes that some keen radio ham would pick up the conversation. Likewise, the conversation allegedly between Prince Charles and Camilla was tuned into via a radio scanner in the bar of a pub in Merseyside —by great coincidence some ten days before the Squidgy conversation was overheard. Three such damaging taped phone calls in the space of ten days . . . Isn't that stretching the laws of coincidence just a little too far?

The two recordings that some two years later became known as the Squidgy Tapes were eventually deposited by the *Sun* in the Midland Bank in Fleet Street for safekeeping until the newspaper's hand was forced by circumstance to "publish and be damned" in August of 1992. The taped conversation that spawned Camillagate was kept secretly by an unnamed member of the public for almost three years before being handed over to Harry Arnold of the *Daily Mirror* in November of 1992. It was made public almost immediately. And while public opinion may be in favor of hurling bricks at the newspapers for revealing such indelicate and utterly damaging material, some heavier artillery should be aimed in the direction of the Security Services. Hutchins and Thompson make the point that whatever the morals of publishing such sensitive royal material, the Security Services were somewhat laid-back, to say the least, when it came to protecting the royal family from scandal.

According to Hutchins and Thompson, Kelvin MacKenzie, editor of the *Sun,* noted:

"It is a very curious thing when three tapes of the royal family are produced within thirteen days. You must think there is probably a plot."
Stuart Higgins, the robust young executive who had delivered Squidgy to the Sun, *spelled out the*

editor's concern in greater detail. "I can't believe that all these things are accidents, and what amazes me is that nobody among the authorities seems to have any kind of interest in conducting an investigation into it," he said. "I know we keep saying that, but they still don't. I would have thought it was a matter of bloody concern, not just a sordid newspaper interest but from a proper investigation interest. I can't understand such adamant failure to investigate it. I've been questioned by the police [but] never been asked by any authority where the tapes come from, where I'd kept them, or if I'd been doctoring them."

Another person who believed that a conspiracy was in progress was Lady Tryon. "What I suggest is that people stop and think deeper about all these so-called revelations," she said. "I believe that republican groups are trying to undermine the country and bring the monarchy down. I suggest the people and the press are being maneuvered by somebody to bring about the monarchy's destruction."

It was also much to Paul's amazement and consternation that despite the obvious risk mobile phones presented to public figures, especially the royals, no technology was implemented—which was available and in common usage in the United States—to protect the users from being overheard. Indeed, when Trevor Kempson and Paul mounted an investigative campaign through the *News of the World* to spur the authorities into taking action about the mobile phone security risk, they got absolutely nowhere at all. And they might not even have got as far as the one article that was published had a few people at British Telecom been successful in urging Trevor to take a holiday at their expense. Obviously because he was overworked. Even to this day, no official action has been taken to alert mobile phone users of the risk they are taking. According to Paul, all mobile phones should come with a government health warning: Use of this article could damage your marriage!

At the very least, the revelations of the private lives of Diana, Charles, Sarah, and Andrew, released with the accuracy of a quartz time capsule, gave the monarchy a gun with which to shoot itself in the foot.

But could republican groups be responsible for stage-managing the downfall of the monarchy? Certainly something other than the hand of fate seems to be operating in the scandals of 1992, but where the truth really lies is almost impossible to fathom. Which is where astrology and the mysterious world of the unconscious come in extremely handy.

I had a dream . . .

In my dream I arrive at Buckingham Palace. There are several cars parked in the forecourt, and there is one—a black sports car—that I know belongs to a great friend of mine, C.D. (Claude, an assumed name, is a high-powered French businessman I am close to in real life and with whom I have had many extraordinary and revealing conversations of both a mystical and future-oriented nature.) I decide to look for

Claude and enter the building. I can see no one, but I can hear voices in the distance. The interior of the building is not like Buckingham Palace as I know it, but more like a temple. There are flags, pillars, shields, and hieroglyphs etched on panels on the walls. Eventually I come to a double door that is slightly ajar. It is opened for me by my friend Claude, who, though surprised to see me, welcomes me in and signals me to stand behind him.

From my vantage point I can see I am in a huge hall, so large that its walls peter out into infinity. At first all I can see are men: some in modern-day suits and others in Jacobean dress.

There is a large table or desk at which I can see the Queen. She is flanked by a member of the clergy in full archbishoplike regalia and a King who resembles George V but in eighteenth-century dress. I try desperately to hear what is being said but cannot decipher anything. But somehow a painting portraying the Declaration of Independence of America on July 4, 1776, comes to mind. The Queen is being shown an ancient piece of parchment. In fact, she is handed the scroll by one frock-coated individual and shown a key by another. A pen is placed in her hand, but she appears unwilling to sign. At that point, the walls of the hall peel back and the whole "set" travels through space at an incredible speed. Images of gargoyles, devils, and biblical scenes involving figures such as Moses and John the Baptist flash past and there are sounds of chanting. (Steven Spielberg couldn't have done it better; indeed the Arc of the Covenant kept coming to mind as I both watched the scene and was moved along with it.) Eventually the tableau comes to rest. We are now on the top of a mountain. The pen is yet again handed to the Queen, who shakes her head. As she does so, everyone disappears and she is left balancing on the pinpoint of the triangular mountain while a giant eagle circles menacingly above her head.

I awoke instantly.

The dream is full of symbolism that I cannot possibly hope to interpret, but it made such an impression on me that, during the course of the last year, I digested a considerable amount of literature on the subject of secret societies and I also met certain individuals who are "switched on" to such matters— or perhaps *illuminated* is a more appropriate word. I have also had other dreamlike experiences that have opened further doors of perception.

Clearly in my dream, the Queen was faced with a choice—to sign or not to sign. And she was given two opportunities to do so. Her decision not to put her signature to the parchment meant that she was isolated and left in a dangerous position. Of course, I was not able to see what was written on the parchment, but my impression was that it involved an agreement made centuries beforehand that the Queen was required to fulfill, and although she was given the choice, in a way she had no choice—she was damned if she did sign and damned if she didn't.

The images of the past that went back to Old Testament days indicated to me that what was at stake was not merely the Windsor dynasty, nor the line of the British monarchy, but a much greater line—and a design that had its origins in a dim and distant past some thousands of years ago.

The eagle is a fascinating image. In Vedic tradition, as in Christianity, the eagle is representative of a messenger from heaven—other schools of thought see the eagle as a symbol of divine majesty. However, the eagle is also a symbol of the United States. Could the eagle circling around the Queen mean that she must bow to a higher power, whether that implies a preordained, God-created plan or the power that rests in America? And the triangular mountain itself—not dissimilar to the one on the front of the American dollar bill . . .

Certainly the links with America throughout the dream are strong, as is the association of ideas: The Declaration of Independence and the Queen being removed to some isolated position—exiled, if you like—indicate to my mind that by not agreeing to the contract drafted some centuries previously, the monarchy would be vulnerable to falling off its pedestal— indeed, it would stand no chance at all of remaining in place and intact.

This may be a somewhat fanciful suggestion, but might it not be that in the greater scheme of things, in which old orders pass away, a monarchy such as Great Britain's not only has no part to play but is a positive threat to the establishment of a new order? The monarchy is an institution that separates Britain not only from the rest of Europe but from the rest of the world. The British Empire may not exist as it did in Victoria's time and the Commonwealth may be disappearing by the day, but England with its great royal tradition is still the envy and admiration of the peoples of the world. Britain is at once a sceptered isle in a silver sea and a sore thumb in the seat of Europe. And in a world that cannot be allowed to get out of control, independence, whether by state, country, or individual, must be staunched.

Since the early 1970s England has been in the process of being swallowed up by Europe. And for the most part, the British don't like it. But with Prime Ministers like Edward Heath and John Major at the helm, we have been persuaded that it is in our best interests. And given the shape of things to come, we really don't have an alternative. Margaret Thatcher was different. No matter how dire her policies in so many respects and the almost criminal damage she inflicted on the arts, the social services, and education, she nonetheless took on the mantle of Britannia and endeavored to keep Britain as independent a nation as possible. And it is far more likely that her removal from power was due to her intransigence over the terms of England's integration with Europe than any internal political power struggle.

To my mind, any stage management of the monarchy's demise is not so much the result of a few isolated but nonetheless powerful groups of republicans, but the unfoldment of a global plan. And this plan fulfills the interests not only of those who believe it is the only way forward for humanity, but of those who believe it satisfies an ancient promise.

I will return to the New Order a little later on, but if the monarchy is already on its way out, whether because it has pressed its own self-destruct button or because it does not fit in with the shape of things to come, can the astrology shed any light on the issue?

On January 30, 1649, at 2:04 P.M., Charles I was executed in London. And thanks to Oliver Cromwell, England became a republic until May 8, 1660, when Charles II was proclaimed King. Now, astrologically, this makes very interesting reading. If we assume that the chart of Charles I's execution is the astrological model for the displacement of English monarchs, we can look to future configurations to see if any patterns are repeated or if any degree areas are picked out.

When it comes to events of a collective nature—of sweeping changes that affect society and the shape of nations—the transpersonal planets—Jupiter, Saturn, Uranus, Neptune, and Pluto—are all-revealing. In the year of Charles I's execution, Uranus and Neptune occupied the same degree of Sagittarius, and Saturn and Pluto were side by side at the opposite point of the zodiac in Gemini. And on the day itself, the moon, Mars, and Venus were all at similar points of Pisces and Virgo—the other two Mutable signs. Now, Uranus and Neptune only form a conjunction every two hundred years or so; a rare event. These planets are synchronous with erosion (Neptune) and revolution (Uranus), and together coincide with the breakdown of established orders and the implementation of new ones. Thus, in 1649 their signature was well and truly on the erosion of the monarchy and the installation of a republic. These two planets also formed a conjunction in Capricorn in 1992, thereby placing the writing firmly on the wall for more than one established institution. Not only this, but Saturn and Pluto—two very disharmonious and disruptive planets—were also at right angles to each other in 1992. Not quite a mirror image of 1649 but near enough to press the point home that any institution that had outlived its usefulness was being served with its notice.

Now, it may be that the axe will finally fall on the monarchy and England will become a republic in 2008 when Pluto enters Capricorn, *the* sign of the Establishment, and both Saturn and Uranus will pick up all-important degree areas on the 1649 execution chart. But in retrospect, 1992, with its chapter of royal scandal, growing doubts over Charles's ability to become the Third, and the great fire of Windsor, will be seen as the beginning of the end of the monarchy—or, perhaps as Churchill would have put it, the end of the beginning of its demolition. The astrological signposts of Uranus and Neptune in Capricorn cannot be misinterpreted. They pointed in the direction of revolution, albeit with no execution and no gunfire.

Also, intriguingly, in 1820 when Uranus and Neptune were previously in conjunction—and in the sign of Capricorn—another Prince of Wales very nearly brought down the monarchy. George IV was crowned in Westminster Abbey on July 19, 1821—but without his "Queen," who made a valiant attempt to break down the doors of Westminster Abbey in order to be crowned with him. George and his Princess, Caroline, did not get on. After their separation, she was exiled abroad and only returned shortly before the coronation. Caroline had the popular support of the people, who considered George a feckless and insubstantial figure. And there was a public outcry when George tried to push through a divorce in 1820. Sadly, Caroline was to die a mere six weeks after the coronation.

As Nick Campion concludes in his book, *Born to Reign:*

> *George (IV) was profoundly unpopular, due to his continued outrageous extravagance during the economic recession which followed the Napoleonic Wars.* [1992–93 also marked the lowest point of recession, certainly in Britain.] *Caroline, on the other hand, partly because of her husband's treatment of her, had the nation's sympathy; she was cheered in the streets of London while her husband was booed and jeered.*
>
> *George must obviously bear personal responsibility for dragging the monarchy down, but the crisis of 1820–21 offers the clearest evidence of a deeper cycle operating in the affairs of the English monarchy . . . Uranus and Neptune had come together in the zodiac, completing one cycle and*

initiating another. These planets were not to meet again until 1992–93.

While compiling the material for this chapter, I asked Nick Campion his views on whether he thought Britain would become a republic. He said that until recently, he doubted it, but an incident that took place in February of 1994 put a rather different complexion on the issue. While being interviewed by Andrew Morton for a forthcoming program for Granada Television on the royals, Nick was asked if he considered Britain would become a republic. At the moment Andrew uttered the question, all the lights in the studio went out.

Nick, like myself, is a great believer in synchronicity—which perhaps requires a little more explanation. Put another way, a separate incident that occurs at the time of another event acts in some strange way as an omen—underlining the importance of the event and adding meaning to it. For example, if I were to receive a letter inviting me to spend six months in New York, and at the moment I read the letter, a news report on the television revealed that the Statue of Liberty had been struck by lightning, I would probably take that as an indication not to go—or to accept but with the clear understanding that New York would be an electrifying experience for me—and probably rather damaging!

In late 1993 there had been a flurry of interest in another strange occurrence involving the royal family.

Horoscope magazine, drawing from an article that had appeared some years previously in an astrological publication, *The Quarterly,* reported that at the time of William's christening, a sudden draft almost blew out the candle being held aloft by Charles. The author, mystic and Jungian, Laurens Van der Post, who was one of William's godfathers and present at the christening, took this to be a sign that there would be a conflict between the Church and the monarchy and that, although the monarchy would survive (because the candle did not go out), there would be a diminution of its significance—its light.

However, when asked to comment further on this mysterious phenomenon, Van der Post strongly denied the candle episode and threatened to sue anyone who suggested any such event had taken place.

My own experience of synchronicity, somewhat predictably perhaps, involved Diana and Charles. In March of 1987 my family and I moved to Hampshire. We had a moving company pack and box all our belongings—which it did with great care and efficiency. Of all our possessions—and there was a wealth of crystal glassware—only one item was damaged—a mug celebrating the marriage of Diana and Charles. Despite being cushioned by a quantity of bubble wrap, the mug had been broken into two pieces—neatly separating Charles and Diana. The significance struck us all.

Given that Nick's experience of the studio lights going out had put the republic issue in an altogether different light for him, I asked when he thought this momentous event would take place. Of three potential years, Nick favors 2017. "This year is shown astrologically to be a time of great instability for Britain." Other strong contenders for the year of the republic are 2001 and between 2007 and 2009.

As Nick points out, Pluto's transit of Capricorn—the sign of law and order and the Establishment—between 2008 and 2024, will have major repercussions on governing bodies across the globe—a prospect reinforced by Uranus's entry into Aries in 2011. Between 2011 and 2017 a tense ninety-degree relationship between these two revolutionary bodies will be in effect. Among other astrological factors, the ending of this tense aspect will coincide with the coming into being of the republic.

Nick believes that William will be the monarch to inherit Elizabeth's crown, and this could well happen in late 2007 or 2008. In December of 2007, both Jupiter and Pluto will be crossing William's Ascendant and expressing the theme of death and rebirth. The following month these two planets will oppose his sun in Cancer. Just as his mother, Diana, experienced a death of her old life as a Sloane Ranger and was reborn as the Princess of Wales when Pluto crossed her Ascendant in 1981, so will William undergo a similar transformation of his identity. I have to add, somewhat sagely, that when Pluto crossed Margaret Thatcher's Ascendant, she also underwent the great transformation: She fell from power.

Nick picked out 2001 as also being significant because Jupiter, Saturn, and Pluto will all be at sensitive points of the Mutable signs, thereby triggering key components of the Charles I execution chart. However, this was by far Nick's least favored period, if only because common sense told him that the toppling of an institution such as Britain's monarchy would take considerably longer than seven years, and in all seriousness could not possibly take place while Queen Elizabeth is on the throne. But then again, who would have thought the Berlin Wall, together with Communism, would have collapsed virtually overnight just before Christmas 1989?

In Nick's view, any change in the monarchy's status will take the form of a compromise whereby Britain will retain the trappings of a monarchy—all the pomp and ceremony that the British do so well—but nonetheless become a republic. Charles will not become King. William will inherit the throne—albeit in a somewhat revamped and less privileged form. And the years in question: 2008/9 for William's ascent to the throne, and 2017 for the advent of the republic. Nick also believes that another way of making the republic acceptable to the British public, and at the same time maintaining the threads of the monarchy, would be to invite a member of the royal family to become President. And the most obvious candidate here—at least for my money—would be Richard, Duke of Gloucester, of whom we shall hear more later.

Cordelia Mansall, another of England's finest astrologers, also pinpoints 2017 as a most significant year for Britain and the monarchy. But she interprets the astrological portents of 2017 as the coronation of William and the return of the Windsors to their former "glory." Cordelia's view is that 1996 will mark the end of an era for the monarchy. The Queen, suffering a great loss, or perhaps some other debilitating experience, will not be able to fulfill her royal duties and will hand over the reins to Charles—but without his being crowned King. This changeover forms a natural bridge between the old style of monarchy and a new one. Cordelia sites Jupiter's position at thirteen Aries—the Midheaven of Charles's chart; the point signifying his life direction, his destiny—and Saturn at zero degree of Taurus (the Queen's sun and Charles's moon) as indicative of the acquisition of power. Jupiter provides the grandiose aspect of "kingship," and Saturn the obligation, duty, responsibility, even the sadness, involved in inheriting such a destiny.

Cordelia sees 2009–10 as years "when the royals have to be subjects of the people"—in other words, this is the time of the republic. But, just as in 1660, there will be a return to the monarchical system in 2017 when William is crowned.

Neither Cordelia nor Nick see Charles being crowned King, although Cordelia does see him taking over the responsibility and trappings of the role of head of state for a while.

I have already fully covered the reasons why I believe Charles will not claim his birthright and some of the nonastrological reasons why I consider Britain must become a republic. But, like my fellow astrologers, I find putting the astrological timing on such an event is tricky. There is just so much material to consider and so many variables. However, I believe that the changeover to a republic—or some major restructuring of the monarchy—will happen before the end of this century and very possibly in 1999.

Pluto's fully fledged entry into Sagittarius in November 1995 will mark a series of global changes and certainly some major developments in the field of communications, but where Britain and the monarchy specifically are concerned, Pluto's arrival in this Mutable sign heralds the start of a series of major links to the chart of the execution of Charles I—"the model for the displacement of monarchs." Throughout 1999, Pluto will be hovering around nine Sagittarius and at the exact opposite point to Pluto in the execution chart. The words *transformation, death* and *rebirth* have been used many times over to describe the significance of this planet, so, if nothing else, the hand on the cosmic clock is pointing to the hour an axe of some sort is primed to fall.

In December of 1998, Neptune will arrive at zero Aquarius, thereby forming a depressively difficult angle to Charles's moon and the Queen's sun. By March of 1999, Saturn will have reached zero Taurus —the same sun-moon position. Mid-July finds Uranus and Saturn at right angles to each other at the same time as a lunar eclipse in Leo touches off yet another sensitive royal degree area. Indeed all the eclipses in 1999 occur on the regal Leo-Aquarius axis. So this is certainly forecast as a summer of discontent for the monarchy, even if the events don't quite eclipse the spectacular happenings of 1992. And if these dark days do not pinpoint a major change in the status quo for the monarchy, then we could look to 2001 when Saturn and Uranus will have reached the twenty-fourth degree of Taurus and Aquarius—the self-same positions that Pluto and Saturn occupied in 1992 and 1993. Somewhat intriguingly, this twenty-fourth degree was exactly rising in the horary chart I set up for the issue of the republic.

I had been working on this chapter in March of 1994 and experiencing considerable difficulty in sifting the wheat from the chaff of the astrological data. There was so much to cover, I couldn't arrive at a conclusion. Then, driving to London one Thursday afternoon, I suddenly realized that I should ask the question of the astrology. So I checked my watch— exactly 2:34 P.M.—and my position—just rounding the Devil's Punchbowl at Hindhead. On my return home I set up a horoscope for that moment, which in the "business" is known as a *horary chart.* What I hoped the chart would give me was a definitive answer to the question: Will England become a republic?

It may be a lot to ask the uninitiated to take on board the notion that a moment in time holds the answer to a question—the signature of the event is in the "stars," so to speak—but, as with so many aspects of astrology, the proof of the pudding is in the eating, and horary charts do produce answers on most occasions and certainly provide food for thought.

At the exact moment I voiced the question, twenty-four degrees of Leo was the Ascendant degree. Not only this, but the moon was rising at precisely twenty-four degrees of Leo. Leo, of course, is the royal sign, which meant that the chart was a valid one—the symbolism reflected the question. For a yes or no answer to my question, the sun (the ruler of the chart) needed to be in aspect to Venus (the ruler of the tenth house, signifying government and rulership). Although the sun was not in close contact with Venus, it was moving towards such a meeting—and without hindrance from any other planet. And Venus was situated in the ninth house, which in horary astrology concerns parliament. There are many other subtleties in this chart which reflect the nature of revolution and reveal huge change, but since this is not an astrological textbook, making mention of them would only complicate the issue. In short, the answer to my question was yes: England will become a republic.

My feelings that the turn of this century will prove to be the time that these enormous changes take place is not only based on the astrology, however. The great sixteenth-century prophet Michel de Nostredame—Nostradamus—earmarked 1999 as the ending of an epoch when there would be tremendous upheaval on a global scale. His prophecies for the future of mankind were published in a book, *The Centuries,* and consisted of a hundred four-line predictions—or quatrains. Leaving aside his terrifying prospect of wars, pestilences, and Antichrists—very similar in nature to the biblical scenarios for the end of the millennium depicted by Daniel and Saint John (Revelations)—Nostradamus made many predictions about the British monarchy.

The difficulty with Nostradamus's predictions, however, is not only that they are written in a mix of old French, Latin, and doggerel, and therefore somewhat challenging to translate, but the four-line stanzas that make up each prediction are not placed in chronological order nor in any thematic sequence. So, although Nostradamus has been uncannily accurate about specific events occurring hundreds of years after his death, many of these prophecies have remained unsolved until the event has actually happened.

The quatrain that gave Nostradamus the equivalent of overnight fame in 1559 was that concerning the tragic death of Henri II of France. When *The Centuries* was published in 1555, much was made of this quatrain and great care was taken by the French royal family that such a prophecy would not be fulfilled.

Le lyon ieune le vieux surmontera

The young lion will overcome the old

En champ bellique par singular duelle:

in a field of combat in a single fight

Dans caige d'or	**In a golden cage**
les yeux	**his eyes**
creuera	**will be pierced**
Deux classes (fractures) *une*	**two wounds in one**
puis mourir	**he then dies**
mort cruelle	**a cruel death**

(Centuries I:35)

On the occasion of the marriage of his daughter, Elizabeth, Henri II took part in the festive jousting at St. Antoine. On the third bout his opponent, the Scottish guard Montgomery, pierced Henri's golden helmet with his lance, which entered Henri's brain just above the eyes. Henri suffered an agonizing death some ten days later. Both men had a lion depicted in their coat of arms.

At the time of Edward VIII's abdication, interpreters of Nostradamus believed they had deciphered another quatrain:

Pour ne vouloir	**For not wanting to**
consentir	**consent**
au divorce	**to the divorce**
Qui puis après	**which then afterwards**
sera cogneue	**will be considered**
indigne	**undignified**
Le Roy des Isles	**the King of the**
sera chasse	**[British] Isles**
par force	**will be forced to flee**

Mis a son lieu   **and one put in his**
que de Roy   **place who has**
n'aura signe.   **no sign of kingship.**

(Centuries 10:22)

Nostradamus does not say *who* did not want to consent to the divorce, but this has been previously thought to refer to the Establishment and/or the British people, who were opposed to the idea of their King marrying the twice-divorced Wallis Simpson. Certainly, in the wake of Edward's failure to win the government's approval of Wallis becoming Queen of England, he was forced into exile abroad. And the one who "had no sign of kingship," his brother, George, was put in his place. However, I think this quatrain makes much more sense applied to a future scenario. Given that Charles and Diana will divorce, if this prophecy is to be translated correctly, the implication is that Charles will not want to consent to Diana divorcing him. Certainly developments over the past two years could be fairly accurately described as undignified. And surely "one who has no sign of kingship put in his place" would more appropriately refer to an individual with no royal blood whatsoever flowing through his veins. So unless the one "put in his place" is a royal bastard, the candidate for head of state must be a president elected by the people. For my money, this quatrain refers to the divorce of Diana and Charles precipitating the whole succession debate—this time in earnest. And, for one reason or another, Charles being pressured to live abroad while a nonhereditary head of state takes over.

Another quatrain that has been ascribed to Edward VIII but also makes more sense applied to Charles is again to be found in Centuries 10.

Le jeune nay	**The young one**
au Règne	**born to the**
Britannique	**kingdom of Britain**
Qu'aura le père	**which his dying**
mourant	**father has**
recommande	**commended to him**
Icelui mort	**Once he is dead,**
Lonole donra	**London will**
topique	**disagree with him**
Et a son fils	**and the kingdom**
le règne	**will be demanded**
demande.	**back from his son.**

(Centuries 10:40)

Two factors are curious about this quatrain. The dying father "recommending" the son, and the mysterious word *Lonole*. When George IV died, the succession automatically passed on to Edward VIII. George did not have to recommend his eldest son for the post—the throne was his birthright. *Recommend* would make more sense applied to a father who put his son forward rather than himself. And dying does not necessarily have to refer to a physical death so much as the renunciation of a role you were born to fulfill. Nostradamus often resorted to anagrams if he wished to make something even more difficult to fathom, so Lonole has been variously interpreted as Oliver Cromwell (Ole Nol was supposedly a French nickname for Oliver), destroyer (from the Greek 'olleon'), and a distortion of London. I cannot offer an explanation for this curious word, but perhaps someone has yet to emerge from the corridors of power whose initials or name itself will fulfill the Nostradamian criteria.

Whether or not these quatrains will turn out to apply to a future scenario when Charles will hand over his birthright to William, who in turn is forced to give up the throne; whether there is indeed a messy divorce after which Charles takes up some foreign diplomatic post or disappears into relative obscurity, Nostradamus and his quatrains cannot be easily dismissed. He was a learned and respected man of his time. If we follow my line of suggestion that what is taking place now in Britain and Europe—if not the three "corners" of the world—is very much part of the unfoldment of the final part of a great plan. Nostradamus's Centuries is clearly much more than a collection of clever riddles.

Nostradamus followed a great tradition of royal astrologers. His grandfather, Jean de San Rémy, was a physician, cabalist, and astrologer—and a member of the court of René d'Anjou. And René d'Anjou was Grand Master of the Priory of Sion. The Priory could be loosely described as a secret society dating back to the time of the Knights Templar. But, like all societies of a similar vein, the roots of its tradition go back much, much further. Part mystical, part political, secret orders have steered the course of history. They still do.

Thousands of years ago, elders and priests handed down forbidden knowledge in the form of myths and legends. While to the uninitiated these myths and legends, like the parables, feed the imagination and the soul but have no basis in reality, to the initiated— through their understanding of, for example, sacred geometry—these stories transmit essential truths.

Plato and Pythagoras were initiated into the Mysteries, and many of their writings, while poetic and philosophical, nonetheless impart very specific pieces of information. To a certain extent now as then, the true initiate, whatever order, group, or society he belongs to, be it the Brotherhood of the Dragon, the Order of the Quest, the Knights of Malta, the Priory, or whatever, is guided to great truths by virtue of his raised and enlightened consciousness as well as being taught and put through a series of ritual initiations.

Baigent, Lee, and Lincoln have done a far better job in their books *Holy Blood, Holy Grail, The Messianic Legacy,* and *The Temple and the Lodge* than I can do here in revealing the workings of such societies as the Priory of Sion, but they confirm my understanding that Nostradamus was part and parcel of a design to keep aloft the tradition and teachings of the Priory.

Nostradamus spent a considerable period of life in the Duchy of Lorraine. This would appear to have been some sort of novitiate, or period of

*probation, after which he was supposedly initi-
ated into some portentous secret. More specifically, he is said to have been shown an ancient and
arcane book on which he based all his own
subsequent work. And the book was reportedly
divulged to him at a very significant place—the
mysterious Abbey of Orval . . . where . . . the
Prieure de Sion may have had its inception . . .*

(Holy Blood, Holy Grail)

By writing his Centuries in the certain expectation
of their enduring popularity, Nostradamus, without
any official link to the Priory, could ensure the perpet-
uation of this knowledge in the event of the demise of
the Priory. In this way, he was entrusted with one of
the most important roles in the history of the Priory:
to become its most enduring mouthpiece. Using the
technique adopted by mystics across the ages, he
publicly addressed anyone and everyone. Yet at the
same time, he concealed the true meaning from all
except those open to perceive such truths. In a sense,
the Centuries have acted as a sort of time bomb in that
the prophecies can only be understood when the time
is right.

Maybe this is just fanciful idea-mongering. Maybe
Nostradamus was merely a gifted clairvoyant and
astrologer who cloaked his forecasts in metaphorical
and grammatical mist in order to escape being hung,
drawn, and quartered by the Inquisition. Maybe it
was just a giant coincidence that his grandfather
moved in the august circles of the French Court,

whose King just happened to be the Grand Master of a powerful secret society. Maybe the Priory of Sion, which is still a functioning order today, is merely a group of individuals who come together to chat about old times and give a helping, charitable hand to each other and worthy causes. And maybe the rumor that certain powerful figures from the world of politics and finance belong to such groups as the Royal Institute of International Affairs and the Trilateral Commission is precisely that—a rumor with no foundation. But what cannot be disputed is that the tide in economic and global affairs generally is by no means a haphazard process but a carefully orchestrated one. And while there are people in positions of great power who appear to govern and rule, they are more truly puppets whose strings are pulled by secret hands.

In 1936, when Edward VIII abdicated the throne, the British public was kept entirely ignorant of the huge chess game being played. Only one week before the abdication took place were the people of Great Britain informed via the press of the serious nature of the relationship between Edward and Mrs. Simpson and the constitutional crisis it posed. I will leave it to A. N. Wilson to elaborate . . .

The reason for the silence of the papers was that the proprietors had been frightened off by the Establishment . . . The Establishment had decided, long before the "abdication crisis," that they would get rid of the King, and they did not wish their plans—for the coronation of the Duch-

ess of York and their tame King-candidate, her husband—to be interfered with by a popular upsurge. Had the abdication crisis happened in 1992, with a free press all commenting on the situation and influencing events as they unfolded, it is difficult to know what would have happened . . . There might have been a surge of republicanism which would have led to the abolition of the monarchy. There might, instead, have been a populist movement to crown Queen Wallis in Westminster Abbey . . . But the press was muzzled in 1936, and so neither thing happened. Instead King George VI and Queen Elizabeth were crowned, and their elder daughter, Lilibet, was groomed for becoming Queen of England.

In his book, *The Rise and Fall of the House of Windsor*, A. N. Wilson categorically states what many would only have dared whisper years ago. The Establishment did not want Edward as King. And so they set about removing him. While some believe Edward's dilettante behavior and his courting of Adolf Hitler made him unacceptable to the Establishment, others maintain that the intent was to destabilize the monarchy in order to bring about its demise. But whatever the real reason behind Edward's abdication, what is clear is that it was no accident, nor a self-inflicted act, but part of a deliberate design.

A. N. Wilson, however, not only questions the notion that there is still an Establishment who can manipulate events to suit its own purposes, but suggests that if there were such a coherent body, the free press would defeat its aims because the voice of the people would have to be heard. However, I would suggest that it is through the very use of the free press that public opinion can be swung this way and that. Journalists still have to bow to an editor's decision, and an editor must still take his lead from a publisher . . . And while there may not be an Establishment as such behind the manipulation of opinion, there is definitely a body of power. And I would hazard a guess that this body believes in a New World Order.

And so the monarchy is being tried in the pages of the free press, and the opinion of the people steered along to its inevitable verdict: Off with its head! Put less dramatically, the concept of a republic is being planted in the British people's consciousness—through the subtle use of television debate and the like—so that the transition from the old status quo to a new one can be made with as little fuss as possible. Indeed, the republic will be the wish of the people.

The year 1994 is clearly a big one for Charles. Without Diana continually eclipsing his star, he can reveal to Britain and the world what a potentially marvelous King he will be. And with Jupiter transiting Scorpio during 1994, he couldn't ask for better astrological help to speed his cause. However, I have my doubts that he will pull it off. Recently Charles used the medium of television to get his voice across to the people. But instead of using the most popular channel and an early evening time slot, he opted for the more cerebral BBC2 and a program transmitted at

10:40 P.M. And instead of coming across as a man wholly accessible to the people, he emerged as a somewhat repressed and arrogant figure. This, sadly, is not the way he is in the flesh. His warmth, humor, and genuine concern for the well-being of individuals and humanity alike are utterly apparent. But he must have lost half the viewers in one fell swoop when he uttered irritably, "Well, if people don't know what I'm on about by now . . ."

But people don't know. They see Charles through the eyes of the media, and he is not a darling of the media. Diana was—still is. And while Charles and the monarchy may already have lost the battle to remain as they are, there is still time to negotiate terms. The jury is still out.

I realize that by putting forward such theories, I run the risk of being accused of adding fuel to the republican fire myself. People may well assume that I advocate the installation of a republic. But I don't. While I believe we must move with the times, and there is a part of me that respects those who chart the way forward, in my heart of hearts I feel the transposition of the British monarchy is too high a price to pay for the advance of civilization and the fulfillment of a grand design.

The value of the British monarchy does not rest only on its function as a major tourist attraction. As A. N. Wilson so beautifully expresses it: "The monarchy is not just a golden bauble on the top of a stone pyramid: It is more like the golden thread running through an entire tapestry. Unpick it, and much more than the thread would be lost." The monarchy may not have the ability to overrule Parliament, but every Member of Parliament, every member of the armed forces, every civil servant, every bishop, must make an oath of obedience to the Sovereign. And, as Spain realized to its cost, a country without a monarchy can, in the wrong hands, become a dictatorship.

When Charles I was pleading his case before Parliament, he made some profound and eloquent statements that are as relevant today as they were in 1649:

> *A king cannot be tried by any superior jurisdiction on earth. But it is not in my case alone, it is the freedom and the liberty of the people of England; and do you pretend what you will, I stand for their liberties. For if power without law may make laws, may alter the fundamental laws of the kingdom, I do not know what subject he is in England, that can be sure of his life or anything that he calls his own . . .*

Of course, there are republics across the world that have not become dictatorships, and the United States, arguably the most powerful country in the world, has achieved its greatness without a monarchy. So why not Britain, too?

What was a few years ago unthinkable is now becoming more than idle speculation. Britain could become a republic, and if I have read all the signs— astrological and otherwise—correctly, the die is already cast. However, there is no reason to believe that the royal family will be exiled to the Outer Hebrides —or wherever.

In *The Rise and Fall of the House of Windsor,* A. N. Wilson suggests the Windsors have "reached the end of the road." However, he does not advocate a republic but a change of dynasty. Pointing out that the Tudors served their country for 126 years and the Hanoverians for 123, the Windsors, at well over 150 years, could be said to be at the end of their natural shelf life. And in order to preserve Britain's perfectly good arrangement between a hereditary monarchy and Parliament, a change of royal family would be the perfect solution.

And the candidate for King? Richard, Duke of Gloucester.

Without going into too much historical detail, the Duke of Gloucester has a legitimate claim to the throne, being a descendant of the Duke of Monmouth, King Charles II's son by his alleged marriage to Lucy Walters. According to Wilson, the fact that Richard of Gloucester is a low-profile, utterly respectable—no trace of scandal—individual would ensure the continuation of Britain's monarchy. However, even Wilson has to admit that it is exceedingly unlikely that the Queen would declare the Duke and his descendants heirs to the British crown. And even more unlikely that there would be a popular uprising.

But Richard of Gloucester, with his Danish wife, would be eligible for head of state were Britain to opt to become a republic. It may be a great British compromise, but it would ensure that Britain does not lose touch with its greatness.

A considerable amount of ground has been covered through the chapters of this book. The mystical has been interwoven with real-life events, and near farcical situations have been sandwiched between issues of a profound nature. We may go on debating whether Charles can or will be King and whether Diana wittingly or unwittingly accelerated the decline of the House of Windsor, but none of us can really be sure what is created by human trial and error and what is the result of some perfectly orchestrated design. I can only speak for myself here, from my own experience as both a frail human being and a traveler in time, that whatever else we may successfully avoid in life, we can never escape an appointment with destiny.

P.S. . . .

This book was well into production by the summer of 1994 when it suddenly became necessary to add a final chapter. Like some strange echo of August 1992, I was yet again on holiday abroad with my children when a major story about the Princess of Wales broke. Actually, the story had broken the Sunday before I left but came to a head as I touched down at Malaga Airport.

On Sunday, August 14, a small story appeared on an inside page of the *News of the World.*

TELEPHONE CRANK
AT THE PALACE

Crank phone calls to a girl pal of Princess Di's former friend, James Hewitt, came from INSIDE Kensington Palace. The "abusive and obscene" late-night calls were made by a woman. They were traced after the victim complained to police, who asked British Telecom to investigate.

Royal police were told and they hushed up the scandal under orders from Scotland Yard chiefs. A senior officer told the victim the calls came from the Palace and persuaded her to keep quiet. A police source said, "It's the hottest potato of all time."

News of the World, August 14, 1994

At the time, I hoped desperately that the calls would turn out to have been made by a Kensington Palace employee, but having worked in Fleet Street for three years and become accomplished at reading between the lines, I suspected Diana herself may well be implicated.

The following Sunday, August 21, in two-inch-thick letters, the headline of the *News of the World* declared DIANA MADE PHONE CALLS TO MARRIED OLIVER.

According to the newspaper, the multimillionaire Islamic art dealer Oliver Hoare began to receive anonymous silent phone calls in September 1992. At their peak there were as many as twenty phone calls a day. More than a year later, in October 1993, at the insistence of his French-born wife, Diana de Waldner, he made an official complaint to the police.

Whoever it is just wants to hear my voice. They keep hanging on as long as I talk. If I put the phone down, they'd just come back. I would be polite and say, "Hello, who's calling? Who's there?" But there was just silence at the other end. It was eerie.

News of the World, August 21, 1994

On Thursday, January 13, 1994, a device that could trace the source of the mysterious calls was finally placed on Mr. Hoare's line by Kensington Police. The first silent call logged that morning was at 8:45, the second at 8:49, the third at 8:54, the fourth at 2:21 P.M., another at 7:55 P.M., and a final one at 8:19 P.M. This pattern was to be repeated to a greater or lesser extent over the following few days. All the calls were traced either to Diana's private line, Charles's private line, Diana's mobile phone, or other private lines at Kensington Palace. On January 19 and upon discovering the source of the calls, Oliver informed the police that he would confront Diana personally. He did and apparently she apologized. But within a matter of days, the calls started up again. This time from public telephone boxes in the Kensington and Notting Hill areas of central London.

Di, worried because eavesdroppers taped the "Squidgy" calls from her mobile phone, still believes that she is safe calling Oliver from outside lines. But she also makes another telltale call—from her sister, Sarah McCourquedale's home. Police decide the situation is "getting out of hand." They pass the problem to Commander Robert Marsh, head of the Royalty Protection Squad—a man who can be trusted to handle sensitive situations tactfully. Marsh briefs a senior Home Office politician about the implications of the "Royal difficulty." The politician, believed to be a minister, advises a senior member of the Royal Household on how the situation should be tackled best. The wheels are set in motion—and there are no more calls to Oliver's home.

News of the World, August 21, 1994

The impact of the *News of the World* article was sensational. It had authenticity and the sort of detail that looked almost impossible to refute. But the following day, an exclusive interview given to journalist Richard Kay by the Princess of Wales appeared in the *Daily Mail* and seemingly exonerated her completely.

WHAT HAVE I DONE
TO DESERVE THIS?

The Princess of Wales has opened her heart to the *Daily Mail* as she faces the most damaging allegations of her life . . .

In conversation with Richard Kay, Diana flatly stated that she had nothing to do with the nuisance phone calls, and the first she heard of them was that very Saturday (August 20) when she was approached by a complete stranger as she left her Chelsea fitness club. Believing the cards were unfairly stacked against her since it seemed she had neither the backing nor the protection of Buckingham Palace—and her friends might well misrepresent her—she decided to take control of events herself and speak directly to the *Daily Mail.*

> From the moment we spoke, it was clear she was extremely distressed. "They are trying to make out I was having an affair with this man or had some kind of fatal attraction. It is simply untrue and so unfair," she told me. "Somewhere, someone is going to make out that I am mad, that I am guilty by association. That mud will stick," she said . . . "I am bemused by this constant attention, photographers follow me constantly at a level of intrusion that I reasonably thought would diminish . . ."
>
> She does, of course, know Mr. Hoare . . . He has long been a friend of Prince Charles and acted as a go-between and honest broker when the royal couple's marriage began to fall apart . . . [But] Diana told me: "He is a friend, he has helped me and I have phoned him."
>
> Again and again she denied she had been responsible for nuisance calls.
>
> The *Daily Mail,* August 22, 1994

Kay went on to refer to further claims by the *News of the World* in which Oliver had stated that in the aftermath of discovering the source of the silent calls, he had shouted Diana's name down the phone and heard the tearful reply, "Yes, I'm so sorry, so sorry. I don't know what came over me." Diana denied such an incident had ever taken place. She also had strong comments to make on the suggestion that the calls only stopped when a Home Office minister approached a senior member of the royal household with what was described as "a clear warning that prosecution would be considered if they continued."

> Diana insisted over and over again that the allegations were false . . . "No one has spoken to me about this matter at any time, no policeman, nobody. I only learned today." . . . She believes the implications of the claims are enormous. "Do you realize that whoever is trying to destroy me is inevitably damaging the institution of monarchy as well?"
>
> The *Daily Mail,* August 22, 1994

After extracting another forceful denial from Diana at the suggestion she had made phone calls from public telephone boxes near Kensington Palace— "You cannot be serious . . . I don't even know how to use a parking meter, let alone a phone box."—Kay went on to ask the Princess about the nature of her relationship with Oliver Hoare.

"I know everyone wants me to be having affairs and this man fits, but it's not true," she said. Then if there was no affair and Diana categorically denied making any nuisance calls, who could have made such distressing calls to Mr. Hoare?

Neither Scotland Yard nor Mr. Hoare have denied the *News of the World* story and it seems clear last night that he did receive calls from telephones to which the Princess would have had access. Unresolved, though, was the central question: Could they have been made by someone else? There has been a claim that a member of the Princess's staff had been quizzed, although the details of this are far from clear. What is certain is that the Princess was in the habit of ringing Mr. Hoare around the time the tapping was being carried out. It is possible that she would have placed the receiver if his wife answered, unwittingly, perhaps, triggering the family's fears that they were receiving nuisance calls.

The *Daily Mail,* August 22, 1994

As the final coup de grâce, the article revealed that Diana's diary entry of appointments appeared to make it impossible for her to be the nuisance caller. According to her diary, at the time of one "silent call," Diana was lunching at Harry's Bar in Mayfair with Lady Stevens, the wife of newspaper proprietor

Lord Stevens. On another occasion, her diary recorded a hair appointment at the studio of Daniel Galvin. Thus, by the end of the *Mail* article, it seemed, indeed, as if there was a conspiracy against Diana—or a serious miscarriage of the truth on the part of the *News of the World* or its sources.

However, by the following day, the tables were turned yet again. Following up the appointments listed in Diana's diary, zealous journalists were soon to discover that on the date of Diana's lunch with Lady Stevens at Harry's Bar, the restaurant was closed. Likewise, staff at Daniel Galvin's salon could neither confirm nor deny whether Diana had an appointment on the date in question.

It was about the third day into the crisis when, taking a break from the searing Spanish sun, I caught the lunchtime news on SKY TV. I remained riveted as person after person appeared to be unable to confirm or deny Diana's presence in their company on specific dates recorded in her diary. The polite lack of support amounted to a silent verdict: guilty. I drove immediately to the nearest news agent to purchase every English paper I could lay my hands on. But I didn't need a newspaper to inform me that this was Diana's biggest crisis. Even the Squidgy Tapes paled into insignificance beside the spectre of Diana not only making three hundred nuisance phone calls but apparently being caught in a network of lies.

Up until this point, Diana's manipulation of people, the media, and the truth had been deemed unthinkable by the public. But here it was in all its glory. No one could have wanted to see her humiliated in this very public way. Nevertheless, her behavior was not unforgivable and it was understandable.

We know from Diana's childhood experience that she was deeply affected by her parents' divorce. She, like many other young children, could not cope with the storm of emotions that raged within her. The feelings of abandonment and rejection were so enormous, she simply cut herself off from them.

This childhood legacy has produced an excessive need to be loved and adored, but at the same time, because she cannot really trust, she cannot find reciprocity in her relationships. Without trust, there can be no real intimacy.

Whether Diana did or did not have an affair with Oliver Hoare is a matter purely for speculation. However, if she made the silent phone calls to anyone, and it now appears that she did, and quite possibly several hundred phone calls over the course of a sixteen-month period, then this would show a certain emotional dependence on the person in question. Most people will admit to phoning someone they have loved and lost in the early stages of bereavement simply to hear the sound of his or her voice, but three hundred . . . ? This could be said to go way beyond the borderline of obsession.

There is almost certainly a huge amount of rage behind a silent phone call, and although this rage would seem to have its focus on the victim, in reality the perpetrator is responding to a vast stockpile of hurt and anger. If one feels abandoned during childhood, every time that person experiences a rejection in adult life, he or she is plunged into the internal reservoir of hurt, and a surge of fear, loneliness, and rejection comes flooding to the surface. As time goes by, hurt piles upon hurt and the scar tissue never has time to heal.

At some point, presumably in the late summer of 1992 when transiting Pluto was exactly squaring her moon—an aspect redolent with emotional turmoil— Oliver must have withdrawn his support from Diana in some way. In a sense he would have been an entirely innocent victim. It's possible he ended up bearing the brunt of Diana's accumulated feelings of rejection and abandonment. If Diana made the calls, she probably told herself countless times not to pick up the phone, but the compulsion would have been stronger than the intention.

An individual who has been emotionally damaged early on can, depending on the level of trauma, become an emotional psychopath. Just like the psychopathic killer who has no sense of guilt or compassion for his or her victims, an emotional psychopath is detached from the emotions that cause him or her to act in bizarre ways. Denial is essential for psychological survival and certainly to keep up appearances in an increasingly threatening world.

Thus, Diana's behavior in the aftermath of the phone call saga is entirely consistent with someone whose first instinct is to head into denial. And while at one time she may have been able to rely on others to support any half-truths or protect her from embarrassment, matters had progressed too far in the Hoare affair to be covered up. Diana had to find some way of coping with the fact that she had been exposed as a possible liar and an alleged phone pest. And at the time, there were real fears that her fragile psyche might not stand up to the experience.

While Diana's academic record was inglorious to say the least, she is intelligent and very shrewd. Since 1992, she has appeared to make increasingly poor judgments, but this is not because she lacks the intelligence to make sensible decisions. On the one hand, she has tended to seek out people who will tell her what she wants to hear, rather than what she needs to hear, so the advice she has received has been counterproductive. In addition, Diana's instability makes it difficult for her to make rational decisions at times. And it is a pattern that is getting worse. At one time, she would have been able to determine the outcome of an action way down the line, but as we can see from the Hoare affair, she may have been quite incapable of realizing that her diary entries of appointments would be checked for their veracity.

Diana's greatest anchor is the telephone. It is the first thing she reaches for in a crisis. The telephone is more than a device for communication with Diana, it is, quite literally, a lifeline. Most people, and certainly most women, explore their feelings with those they are close to in order to get their bearings on a situation, but this process used to excess reveals a loss of sense of self. Diana, like many people who are in deep pain, looks outwards for an emollient. She reaches out to other people. But the real healing demands an inward journey, and it can only be accomplished alone.

In many ways, Diana's ability to talk about her unhappiness is a positive factor, but it is only a first step toward a resolution. Her response is still an "if-only, poor-me" reaction to her life's events: If only someone would really love me, I would be fine, but love and happiness elude me. Why me? What have I done?

Comparisons have been made between Diana and Marilyn Monroe. Marilyn's inability to find her real self in the midst of everyone else's projection of her eventually led to her death—accidental or deliberate, we shall never know for sure. But I believe a more fitting parallel would be Jackie Kennedy. Like Diana, Jackie was the most feted and photographed woman of her generation, but she fell from her pedestal when she married Aristotle Onassis. Stories of her legendary shopping sprees and other material indulgences drew criticism from every corner of the globe and her popularity quickly waned. After Onassis's death, she became a respected book editor and found happiness, fulfillment, and security in a life bound by her career, her work in the arts, and her beloved family. By the time of her death in 1994, she had not only regained her place as First Lady in the hearts and souls of all

Americans, but ensured her place among the immortals upon Olympus.

And Diana should have followed her lead. Maybe she will. There is still time.

Princess Diana is among a rare group of people who have carved their signature on a century. At this point in time, it may seem as if she is a fallen idol, but despite the opinions aired in this book, she is still a diamond of shimmering beauty in a world that needs every bit of brightness it can get.

Diana is still very much in my heart and there have been many times in the past two years when I have thought about picking up my pen and writing to her. If I had, this is what I would have said.

Dear Diana,

It is a long time since we have spoken, but you have been in my thoughts often, most especially during this August when the twists and turns of events must have plummeted you to a nadir you had not thought possible. But, as they say, the only way on from here is up—and you have more than enough courage to pull yourself back from the brink.

Astrologically, 1992 and 1993 looked to be the greatest term of trial for you. To be specific, Pluto had reached a point in your chart where it formed a Grand Cross with three other planets. The moon and Venus —both pinions of your femininity, the inner you, and your love life—were under tremendous pressure. On the one hand, such an alignment could have brought someone very special into your life—a sort of fateful encounter—evoking all sorts of passionate feelings, and on the other hand, you could have felt utterly pulled apart by such events. Uranus and Neptune—your old "friends"!—were also much in evidence. They were at the very base of your chart, which is often coincident with a change of location or change of job, and it certainly makes you feel uprooted and unsure of your bearings. Anyone would have felt unstable on these aspects and prone to losing her footing on occasion.

I remember wondering whether you would stand the pressure, but you did. You have lived to tell the tale, so to speak. However, as you must know, you still face some tests, and you will need to be as prepared as possible for them, as centered as you can be.

Do you still have the book I sent you at the end of 1991—*Divine Encounters*? If you haven't managed to read it yet, it might give you a helpful perspective on what you have been through and where you are headed. I would never have written *Divine Encounters* without going through the most intensely painful experience myself. I didn't want the experience, but in the end I came to view what had happened to me as purposeful. In fact, it changed everything.

When, in 1990, my world fell apart, I had to find a way of coping with it all. To begin with, I looked to outside sources for help. The hurt was so great, I had to keep moving all the time. I filled every day with constant activity, only stopping when I could escape exhausted into sleep. I couldn't bear to be on my own. I was literally terrified of what those feelings would do to me if I was left alone with them. I thought I might go mad. But eventually I came to understand that I had to meet the pain in order to preserve my sanity. And it became the catalyst of everything good that has since happened to me.

In *Divine Encounters* I describe this journey into

that inner darkness as Persephone's journey because she was the goddess of the Underworld. And, although this is not very easy to put across in a few words, perhaps you can most easily relate what you are currently going through as the journey through the Valley of the Shadow of Death. It may seem terrifying and you may have to confront all sorts of phantoms from the past and feelings and events you would rather forget about. But to meet them consciously is like bringing a beacon of light to bear on the darkness—it diminishes the hold they have on you.

Now, this may sound as though it is the sort of thing you need a psychologist to take you through— and I'm not saying that a good one wouldn't help—but ultimately it's you who must make the understandings, you who must make the journey to awareness. And one of the ways you can do this is by recognizing that every time you meet an experience that brings up all the old fears and all the old patterns of behavior that help you cope with those fears, you must use the pain as a helping hand to push you through a doorway into a new space. That way you create a new route; you don't have to keep going down the same old track. Does this make sense?

Put another way, the more you use the raw material of a painful experience, and the more you perceive events as a stepping stone rather than a stumbling block, the more the darkness and the sense of being persecuted will fall away.

When you put your thoughts across in the *Daily Mail,* you said you believed "they" were trying to damage you and that whoever sought to destroy you was intent on damaging the institution of the monarchy. Well, you may have a point. Perhaps, indeed,

there are certain people in positions of power who
believe you are a loose cannon on the deck of the royal
family, and if you could be pushed over the brink, it
would solve a lot of problems. Were this to be true,
what could you do?

First and foremost, of course, you must be strong
within yourself — not vulnerable to getting blown this
way and that. And you can do this by taking on board
what I've said earlier. But, practically speaking, the
original intention of retiring from public life was
probably along the right lines.

If you compare yourself to other women who have
achieved megalithic fame, those who have endured
have retired at their peak. The myth is always more
powerful than the reality . . . I could be wrong, but it
seems as though you have decided on a policy of
fighting fire with fire and maintaining a high profile,
and although I am a great advocate of such tactics, in
this case I think it is backfiring on you. I imagine the
Establishment can still pack a powerful punch, and
recent events must have shown you that you tend to
come off worse in any skirmish. Take a long, hard look
at what you ultimately want from life, and if, as you
said all those years ago, it's a happy family life and
someone to really love and be loved by, are you going
about it the right way? If you honestly believe you
are — and obviously there are many factors I know
nothing about — then you must continue on your
chosen path. But if there is a shadow of doubt, then
perhaps acquiescence is indeed the better part of
valor.

As we draw to the end of 1994 and throughout
1995, Pluto yet again comes center stage of your
chart. Using it correctly — and this demands all the
inner work on yourself that I was talking about
earlier — you could bring about the biggest personal

transformation of your life. Remember that image of the phoenix rising out of the ashes? Well, here it is again. However, the obverse side to this same planetary theme is a transformation of a less welcome variety. Instead of you empowering yourself, you could be manipulated on a scale you have not yet experienced. You may not know this quote by Rodney Colin, but it is powerful and I think about it a lot in regard to my own life: "Death and transformation are man's unchosen and unchangeable fate. All that he can choose and change is consciousness. But to change this is to change all." Pluto is a great eliminator — a great stripper away of things we really don't need. And the moment you let go, the moment you stop resisting, becomes the moment you are released; the moment you move onto a new and better, more fulfilling stage of life.

You are clearly a great soul, Diana. Since you became engaged to Charles in 1981, you have lit up the world's stage and become one of the most important female icons of the twentieth century. You always believed you had a spiritual purpose to fulfill, and you have found aspects of this in your work already. But what you may not have realized is that your life is a spiritual path in itself. Every experience, especially the difficult ones, takes you that little bit further. There is a choice to be made before the spring of 1995, and going inside yourself will help you make it.

The fork in the road next year could take you on to the kind of life you have always wanted. You will be free to find the right person, free to have more children — free both in the sense of being divorced and free in a psychological way. Indeed, by the time you reach 1999, you have a relatively clear field, and if you have not remarried by then, this is the time to go for it. Cancerians have a way of refusing to let go of anything—people, position, power, whatever—but in the end, if you keep hanging on, you become weighted down by so much excess baggage, you can't move a step forward and you are much easier to push over. So think about shedding the past—every which way—and moving as fast as you can into a brighter future. You deserve it. And although it seems as though other people are holding you back, they're only the mirror of your own projections.

You have so much to look forward to, Diana. Just a few more stepping stones to go. Don't look back. Look to the future.

With love from

Penny
September 22, 1994

On September 23, Diana announced her return to public life.

ASTROLOGY
What's What and Who's Who

A Layman's Guide to Astrology

Astrology is a very complex language of symbolism and therefore difficult to put across to the uninitiated. However, here are some essential parts of the cosmic puzzle.

WHAT'S WHAT

THE ASCENDANT *(also known as the RISING SIGN):* The sign rising above the horizon at birth. This is considered equally as important as the sun sign in the way of describing the personality—the persona, if you like. It can be most easily understood as the doorway to the personality—the cover of the book.

ASPECTS: The angles formed between one planet and another. The aspects are possibly the most important factors of all in astrology. Whether interpreting a birth chart of a person or that of a nation or an event, the aspects reveal much more than the signs of the zodiac. Likewise, in relationships, comparing the angles between one person's planets and the other's gives a dynamic impression of the relationship.

Challenging aspects include:

The conjunction—two planets side by side.

The square—two planets 90 degrees apart.

The opposition—two planets 180 degrees apart—on opposite sides of the zodiac.

Harmonious aspects include:

The trine—two planets 120 degrees apart

The sextile—two planets 60 degrees apart.

THE DESCENDANT: The sign setting on the horizon at birth. This part of the zodiac colors the types of relationships the individual experiences. Often the zodiac sign that is setting is the sun or Ascendant sign of the partner.

THE COMPOSITE CHART: A chart of a relationship based on the halfway points of each partner's planets and houses.

THE HOUSES: In the same way that there are twelve signs of the zodiac, the horoscope is divided into twelve areas—or houses. The first house begins at the Ascendant point, and the others follow on counterclockwise. Each house describes an area of life.

FIRST HOUSE: The persona. The physical

characteristics of the individual. His up-front personality.

SECOND HOUSE: Security—financial and emotional resources.

THIRD HOUSE: Communication.

FOURTH HOUSE: Home and family. The ancestral roots. One of the parents—usually the father.

FIFTH HOUSE: The creative center. Children, the child within. Love affairs.

SIXTH HOUSE: Obligations, duties, work. Well-being—physical, mental, and psychological.

SEVENTH HOUSE: Love, relating, and intimate partnerships.

EIGHT HOUSE: All that is taboo in life. Sex, death, and financial, emotional, and spiritual exchange.

NINTH HOUSE: Far horizons. The higher things of life.

TENTH HOUSE: The role in life. Aims and aspirations. Describes one of the parents—usually the mother.

ELEVENTH HOUSE: Friendships. Joint creative ventures. The capacity to give and receive.

TWELFTH HOUSE: The unconscious, all things spiritual.

THE MIDHEAVEN: The sign directly overhead at birth—the very highest point of the zodiac. This area describes the aims and aspirations of the individual and his role in life. The sign on the Midheaven and the sign at the opposite point is also known as the parental axis because it reveals the type of parenting experienced and sometimes the astrological signs of one or both parents.

THE PLANETS

THE SUN: (Astronomically speaking, the sun is, of course, the star that our solar system revolves around, but for the sake of expedience, we shall refer to it here as a "planet.") The sun and the sign it is placed in describes the personality type. Rather like belonging to a nation, we each have a national identity—we are American, British, or French, for instance, and therefore share many national characteristics with our fellow men. Yet, aside from our national identity, we are unique individuals. The rest of the chart—the Ascendant sign, the sign in which each of the planets is placed, and all the aspects—gives us our individuality.

THE MOON: (The moon, of course, is also not a planet but a satellite of Earth. However, for our purposes here, we shall refer to it as a "planet.") The moon describes our emotional response. The moon, as the great feminine principle, also reveals our experience of mother and mothering. In a man's chart, the moon reveals the kind of woman to whom he is emotionally drawn, and the sign in which the moon is placed is often the sun, moon, or Ascending sign of his partner.

MERCURY: This planet symbolizes communication. The way we think and speak and communicate our ideas and feelings.

VENUS: The planet associated with love and affection. In a woman's chart, Venus describes the way she expresses her femininity and her sexuality. In a man's chart, Venus indicates his way of loving and expressing affection and also the type of woman to whom he is sexually attracted.

MARS: The planet of action and desire. In a woman's chart, Mars indicates her physical nature and the kind of man to whom she is sexually drawn.

JUPITER: Jupiter is the planet of good fortune. This planet also reveals the individual's capacity to find success and his intellectual, philosophical, and spiritual leaning.

SATURN: Saturn represents duties and obligations. This planet is notorious for producing difficulties and restrictions that, in the end, turn out to be the very factors that make us infinitely better and more substantial individuals.

THE OUTER PLANETS

URANUS: The planet of change and upheaval. When this planet contacts the sun, moon, Venus, or Mars, the individual will be unorthodox and unstable in the area of life in question. On the plus side, this planet produces exceptional and unusual characteristics.

NEPTUNE: The planet of mysticism and illusion. When this planet contacts the sun, moon, Venus, or Mars, the individual will have strong artistic and spiritual gifts, yet he or she also has the capacity to be an escapist and self-deluded.

PLUTO: The planet of transformation. When this

planet aspects the sun, moon, Venus, or Mars, it generates passion and volcanic situations.

THE SIGNS OF THE ZODIAC

ARIES (*Fire, Cardinal*): Assertive, headstrong, ambitious, self-motivated—a very macho sign.

TAURUS (Earth, Fixed): Practical, sensuous, dogmatic, resistant to change. Seeing is believing to Taurus.

GEMINI (Air, Mutable): Adaptable, mercurial, mind over emotion. Fears commitment. The zodiac's great communicator.

CANCER (Water, Cardinal): Sensitive, imaginative, artistic, manipulative. Very self-protective—believes the sideways swipe is the best form of defense.

LEO (Fire, Fixed): Passionate, regal, dominating, proud. The drama queen of the zodiac.

VIRGO (Earth, Mutable): Painstaking, anally retentive, discriminating, analytical. Never takes no for an answer.

LIBRA (Air, Cardinal): Fair-minded, indecisive, narcissistic, beauty-loving, stylistically correct. The diplomat of the zodiac.

SCORPIO (Water, Fixed): Deep, suspicious, enigmatic, loyal to the death, and passionate. Not a sign to be underestimated.

SAGITTARIUS (Fire, Mutable): Fun, successful, inconsiderate, immoderate. The globe-trotter and freedom merchant of the zodiac.

CAPRICORN (Earth, Cardinal): Practical, strategic, power-loving, domineering. Neither a pushover nor a hundred-meter sprinter—more a marathon runner.

AQUARIUS (Air, Fixed): Far-seeing, altruistic, intractable—always right. A brilliant advocate when it comes to proving that black is white.

PISCES (Water, Mutable): Mystical, compassionate, dreamy, neurotic. The zodiac's great escapist.

WHO'S WHO

QUEEN ELIZABETH
April 21, 1926; 1:40 A.M. BST; London
A sun TAURUS. Ascendant: CAPRICORN. Midheaven: SCORPIO. Moon: LEO.

THE PRINCE OF WALES
November 14, 1948; 9:14 P.M. GMT; London
A sun SCORPIO. Ascendant: LEO. Midheaven: ARIES. Moon: TAURUS.

THE PRINCESS OF WALES
July 1, 1961; 2:00 P.M. BST; Sandringham
A sun CANCER. Ascendant: LIBRA. Midheaven: LEO. Moon: AQUARIUS.

THE DUKE OF YORK
February 19, 1960; 3:30 P.M. GMT; London
A sun PISCES, Ascendant: Leo. Midheaven: ARIES. Moon: SCORPIO.

THE DUCHESS OF YORK
October 15, 1959; 9:03 A.M. GMT; London
A sun LIBRA. Ascendant: SCORPIO. Midheaven: VIRGO. Moon: ARIES.

PRINCE WILLIAM
June 23, 1982; 9:03 P.M. BST; London
A sun CANCER. Ascendant: SAGITTARIUS. Midheaven: SCORPIO. Moon: CANCER.

PRINCE HARRY
September 16, 1984; 4:20 A.M. BST; London
A sun VIRGO. Ascendant: CAPRICORN. Midheaven: SCORPIO. Moon: TAURUS.

EDWARD VIII
June 23, 1894; 10:00 P.M. GMT; London
A sun CANCER. Ascendant: AQUARIUS. Midheaven: SAGITTARIUS. Moon: PISCES.